Russian Absurd

NORTHWESTERN WORLD CLASSICS

Northwestern World Classics brings readers
the world's greatest literature. The series features
essential new editions of well-known works,
lesser-known books that merit reconsideration,
and lost classics of fiction, drama, and poetry.
Insightful commentary and compelling new translations
help readers discover the joy of outstanding writing
from all regions of the world.

Daniil Kharms

Russian Absurd

Selected Writings

Translated from the Russian by Alex Cigale

Northwestern University Press ✦ *Evanston, Illinois*

Northwestern University Press
www.nupress.northwestern.edu

Printed in the United States of America

10 9 8 7 6 5 4 3 2 1

Library of Congress Cataloging-in-Publication Data

Names: Kharms, Daniil, 1905–1942, author. | Cigale, Alex, translator.
Title: Russian absurd : selected writings / Daniil Kharms ; translated from
    the Russian by Alex Cigale.
Other titles: Northwestern world classics.
Description: Evanston, Illinois : Northwestern University Press, 2017. |
    Series: Northwestern world classics
Identifiers: LCCN 2016047114| ISBN 9780810134577 (pbk. : alk. paper) |
    ISBN 9780810134584 (e-book)
Classification: LCC PG3476.K472 A2 2017 | DDC 891.784209—dc23
LC record available at https://lccn.loc.gov/2016047114

To my grandparents,
Matvei and Basia Flaxman.
For raising me.

CONTENTS

Selected Prose from the Middle Years (1933–1938)

Selected Prose from the Late Years (1938–1941)

Selected Poems (1927–1939)

Daniil Kharms was the pen name of Daniil Ivanovich Yuvachev (1905–1942). With his friend, the poet Alexander Vvedensky, Kharms cofounded the OBERIU, a group of second-generation Russian Futurist or Absurdist writers active in the 1920s and 1930s. Not permitted to publish his mature work in Stalinist Russia, he survived for a time by composing poems for children. At the beginning of World War II, he was arrested (a second time) on the absurd charge of espionage and, feigning insanity to avoid summary execution, starved to death in a psychiatric hospital during the Nazi siege of Leningrad. Most of his writings survived only in notebooks, rescued fortuitously from a burned-out building by a friend and fellow OBERIU member, the philosopher Yakov Druskin. His short sketches, illegally circulated in Russia after the war, influenced several generations of underground writers who broke into the mainstream with the fall of the Soviet Union.

Humor and horror, Eros and Thanatos, degradation and sadomasochism jostle one another, side-by-side, in these stories and poems. Kafkaesque and Chekhovian situations and motifs from Pushkin and traditional Russian fairy tales are recognizable in Kharms's sparse prose, yet they appear diseased, stripped down to their bare essentials, as if contorted by the terror of impending arrest and doom. Covering the entire range between the merely unpleasant, the disturbing, and the hilarious, his protoexistentialist works succeed in bearing, if only tangentially, remarkable witness to the unspoken and unspeakable reality of life under Stalin.

✦

Kharms's work may already be familiar to the reader through one of his inventions: his "old woman" (*starukha*) has become engraved in the cultural hive mind. (In one of her better known incarnations, she is seen blithely falling, over and over, out of various windows.) Kharms's most substantial contribution to the ancient Russian cultural meme—his absurd blending of the fairy tale "old crone" or Baba Yaga, Alexander Pushkin's countess in "The Queen of Spades," and Fyodor Dostoevsky's pawnbroker in *Crime and Punishment*—finds her fullest expression in his longest, late-in-life short story "The Old Woman" ("Starukha," 1939), recently adapted for the stage by Robert Wilson, starring Mikhail Baryshnikov and Willem Dafoe.

Kharms's own clown/jester/buffoon persona, however, rightfully transcends any one of the ready-made Western stereotypes we have slotted him in for—the silly Edward Lear–like British humor, vaudevillian slapstick, Beckettian minimalism, Bauhaus cabaret—for the simple reason that his "holy fool" also happens to speak the pathetically simple truth to Soviet power. In "Let us look out the window" (1930), a piece of Futurist mini-theater—its "characters" are a human being, a bolide, and a pitcher—the human being idiotically intones: "So I go to the food cooperative and say: Give me that can of sardines over there. And they tell me: We have no sardines, these cans are empty. And I tell them: Why are you pulling my leg? And they tell me: It's not our idea. So whose idea is it? It's due to the shortages, because the Kyrgyz have rustled away all the split-hoofed ungulates. So are there any vegetables? I ask them. No vegetables either. All bought up. Keep quiet, Grigoriev."

"Getting" Kharms, I think, requires cultivating a visceral sense of the sociopolitical-cultural context of the repressions and deprivations of the 1920s and 1930s, and the suppression of Kharms and his immediate circle, the "OBERIU" (short for *Ob'edinenie real'novo iskusstva*, the tongue-in-cheek "Association for REAL Art"). The OBERIU had assumed, in their generation, the "Slap in the Face of Public Taste" mantle of the Russian Futurists, literally adopting Kazimir Malevich's encouragement to them as their motto—"Go and stop progress!" After their theatrical zaum-based (or "transrational," "beyond the mind"), Dada-like performances were banned in 1927, Kharms continued to write theatrical pieces, omitted here for the sake of brevity, most famously *Elizaveta Bam*, and to work in the children's theater. (His work consistently makes no distinction between prose and poetry, also incorporating elements of play. Due to space limitations, I was unable to include his quite substantial work in the theater, both Futurist and children's.)

Kharms's artlessness, in accordance with our age, is an anti-art, an insistence that genuine art is autonomous from the "real world" rules of logic, and that meaning is to be found in the objects and words themselves, outside of any practical function. In resisting such commodification and utility, the independent position of the artist constitutes a very "real world" critique of modernity. Strictly at odds with the state's de rigueur conventions of socialist realism, this placed Kharms and his associates under, as it were, a suspended death sentence.

✦

The minimalism of Absurdism is tautological, taking a perverse and morbidly dry pleasure in stories that, like much of life, go nowhere, a very literal practice of the idea that art "makes nothing happen" (think here of W. H. Auden's similar disenchantment of the same historical period). Minimalism as insufficiency of the word qua communication was already in the air when Kharms came of age in the 1920s, during the end stage of Russian Futurism. Such conceptual handling of language had already been brought to its logical conclusion in Vasilisk Gnedov's "Poem of the End" (1913), a blank page that was supposed to be acted out gesturally, and the Constructivist poet Ilya Selvinsky's poem "Report" (1921), essentially a record of the carrying out of an execution (which included the poet's self-reflexive commentary on the subject, placed under the poem beneath a square root sign).

Thumb-twiddling boredom, repetition, hoaxes, and other violations of expectations in evidence here are dissonant and discomfiting in themselves. Elsewhere, Kharms strikes an even more distasteful and offensive pose, an *épatage* (from the French "*épater la bourgeoisie*," or shock the bourgeoisie) that practically wallows in degradation and self-abasement. Explaining his "program," he wrote: "I am interested only in pure nonsense, only in that which has no practical meaning. I am interested in life only in its absurd manifestation. I find heroics, pathos, moralizing, all that is hygienic and tasteful abhorrent . . . both as words and as feelings." In some of his other work, we may find a precedent, for example, for the Theatre of Cruelty;

but there is also, in his depictions of the minutiae of daily life (*byt*), a precedent for the postmodernist, documentary yet paradoxically ironic approach of the Moscow Conceptualist artists and poets of the 1970s who acknowledged Kharms as an essential influence.

One of them, Ilya Kabakov, wrote: "Contact with nothing, with emptiness, makes up, we feel, the basic peculiarity of Russian conceptualism...."* Kharms was similarly central for the postwar generation of nonconformist poets of the 1950s and 1960s (Kropivnitsky, Nekrasov, Satunovsky, Kholin, Sapgir, Eremin, Khvostenko, to name just a few) as well as for the Russian Minimalist poets of the 1970s and 1980s. Just to enumerate some of his aesthetic (that is, anti-aesthetic) values: plain speech, written as it is spoken, folksy simplicity, *byt*, but also the spiritual values of Absurdism—the ridiculous as a reaction and an alternative to revulsion and resignation before an absurd age.

✦

Another key to these writings is the Kharmsian whimsical narrative "I" and his many heteronymous stand-ins—the Grigorievs, the Myshins, the Pronins, the Kuznetsovs—all of them objects of defilement and self-abasement. These "perversions of self" may be viewed through the lens of Michel Foucault's "biopower," the state's subjection of the body to absolute control through its exercise of the right to punish (and not publish), a secular equivalent of the usurpation of God's will on earth. (I have written elsewhere of this spiritual foundation of Kharms's work, in the contexts of minimalism and of his fellow Absurdist Alexander Vvedensky's "prison prose.") The Lacanian psychoanalytic of the "abject," the sadomasochistic dyad inherent in Kharms's oft-repeated and vicious attacks on children, women, the old, and mankind in general, is reminiscent of W. C. Fields's comical persona. (One can only imagine the bitter irony inherent in the fact that Kharms owed his very physical existence to his "official position" as a children's writer!)

* Mikhail Epstein, *After the Future: The Paradoxes of Postmodernism and Contemporary Russian Culture* (Amherst: University of Massachusetts Press, 1995), 200.

However, such seething nihilism doesn't preclude a spiritual dimension, it makes it necessary, something I believe to be true of all minimalist practice. And it is this particularly that will likely remain most incongruous to contemporary anglophone readers. How is it possible to reconcile nihilism (I would argue Kharms was not a nihilist) and make it coherent with, and even motivated by, a personal conception of God? While the folk and Russian Orthodox contexts that are particularly evident in the writings of his friend Alexander Vvedensky (who was a genuinely religious person) and in the content of Kharms's irreverence (he was the son of the religious mystical philosopher Ivan Yuvachev and seemingly an irrepressible person) are outside the scope of this introduction, it is fitting to end by noting that Kharms falls squarely within the Russian tradition of the *yurodivy*, the "holy fool," even to the point of feigning insanity to avoid arrest. I believe that in this naive and sacred ethnographic role, as court jester and sad clown, Kharms (who variously signed himself as Harms, Charms, Shardam, Dan Dan, etc.) can tell us more about the spirit of his, and our, age than the millions of lives and deaths that became (to paraphrase the heartless tyrant) merely a statistic.

✦

The point I would like to make here is that our reading of Kharms in the West has so far been constrained, accounting I believe primarily for the negativist aspects of Russian Absurdism, and not at all for its "afterlife," and that a fuller consideration of his work might be facilitated if we were to pay particular attention to Kharms's development as a writer over the short span of some decade and a half of creative life. So that the development I speak of become self-apparent, the structure of the present book follows as much as possible a strictly chronological order. The chapters that emerge, corresponding roughly to the "Early," "Middle," and "Late," might also be provisionally titled "The Theatre of Cruelty," "The Theatre of the Absurd," and "Protoexistentialism." The interspersed brief biographical sections, taken from Kharms's notebooks, diaries, and letters, are intended to cement a more personal relationship with the author, as well as to establish connections between his creative output and the circumstances and events of his life. These section breaks also provide "pacing" as it were, a sense of a life lived, as well as the mileposts in Kharms's biography that can be mapped over to his writing: the initial suppression of the OBERIU (late 1920s), the breakup of his first marriage and his exile to Kursk after the first arrest (1931–32), and the growing desperation of his final years (late 1930s). I have tried here to briefly represent each of the different types of materials (diaries, notebooks, letters, one of his NKVD confessions). Kharms's poetry, also arranged chronologically, offers, at the end, a summation.

It seems to me that, as Kharms's work matures, the elements of protoexistentialism present in all his writings emerge to the fore. My argument here is that we must take Kharms and Russian Absurdism "more seriously," as a species of protoexistentialist writing within which context Kharms, Vvedensky, and their circle may be viewed as essentially metaphysical poets. In closing, I once again wish to emphasize the afterlife of Kharms's oeuvre, being a widely acknowledged influence on the postwar revival of the Russian avant-garde in its experimental, unofficial, nonconformist manifestations— Kharms as a patron saint to the Minimalists and Conceptualists of the 1960s and 1970s. There is something about Kharms that is emblematic of the condition of the Russian soul, for lack of a more precise word, and thus of our own modern condition. In this, he may well be thought of as a worthy member of the postwar generation of existentialist writers—Sartre, Beckett, and Camus—and (it is my hope) enlisted in the canon of world literature among their ranks.

✦

A note on my practices as both a translator and arranger. There often being no "equivalents" between languages and cultures, I find it sometimes necessary to translate the same term in several variants. One typical instance of this is the Russian "*starukha*," not just "old woman" but, in its sarcastic tone and complex of associations, also "hag," "crone," or, perhaps less acerbically, "the old crone." Similarly, it is an established practice of Russian literary classics that the character names bear significance. So for example with Myshin, who makes an appearance twice in our pages and whose name I have "translated" as Mouseman. In such instances, I have tried to be consistent in my practice of listing the transliterated name or word in brackets the first time it appears.

Additionally, I have found it commonplace that the less context-aware reader of a text in translation often requires some basic elaboration of the original. For example, a Russian reader is implicitly aware of certain social realities, such as the typical living arrangements of the communal apartment (private apartments that had been confiscated and subdivided into separate "rooms" with shared kitchens and bathrooms) and its concomitant lack of privacy as a concept, without an understanding of which the course of events and the characters' thought processes may lack coherence. This is also relevant to certain conventions of linguistic structure and thought, and the established usages of storytelling and writing.

Of the many structural differences between our source and target languages, the following bear notice. In Russian, the subject, object, and sometimes even the verb of a sentence may be implied, and an entire phrase elided and omitted. In English, these all require being named. One relevant note is that such simple phrases as "look into the water" ("Morning" and "How easy it is . . . to become lost in insignificant details") often have an implied secondary figurative meaning, in this case, referring to the use of water in divining the future.

Another primary structural difference is the practically untranslatable nature of many complex Russian verbs (agglutinative or fusional), stringing together the root with prefixes and suffixes to express time, duration, relationship, conditional statement, tone, gender, etc., requiring in English the awkward piling on of prepositions, possessives, and auxiliary verbs. A further complication is the typical use of the passive construction and the more flexible subject-verb order which allow for certain nuances of tone and shading. All these structural differences also reflect on the culturally and socially conditioned reality, permitting, for example, for things to be stated vaguely. Ambiguity, innuendo, and multiplicity of implied meanings is always at play in Russian, and in all such instances, the translator into the very precise English is forced to, more or less, "spell things out" and at least in part "unpack" meaning.

All this extends to certain literary conventions, for example the standard Russian practice of leaving poems untitled (indicated in a table of contents by first line only). Somewhat similar is the greater ease of shifting between tenses, from the past tense of the narration to the more immediate and effective present tense, to emphasise the action, indicative of the more immediate rooting of these tales in the oral tradition. Lastly, one must always keep in mind that this work survived primarily in notebooks; written as it was "for the drawer," without any hope for a reader or audience, it constitutes a kind of private language and examination of thought processes, so that reconstructing it requires some conjecture regarding intended order, completeness, appearance on the page, etc. For example, paper often being in short supply, every inch of it may have been covered and things "pushed together."

Above all else, my intent here has been, while remaining faithful to the original, to produce to the greatest extent possible colloquially fluid English texts, that is, inexact equivalences rather than reproductions or literal translation, this often requiring at least a partial interpretation of authorial intent.

✦

A final note about the ordering and structuring of the material. The separation of the early, middle, and late periods I have identified here is necessarily imprecise, and any slight overlapping is intended to reflect the quite real nature of transitional phases (in Kharms's case, each lasting roughly two years). As I've already noted, and as I believe the work here reflects, his first arrest, interrogation, signed confession, and exile (1931–33) produced a crisis (heretofore unknown degree of isolation, inability to obtain work and food, and a general sense of impending doom) that expressed itself in a reduced output characterized by an almost single-minded rumination upon such abstractions as number theory and infinity.

The last phase of his life and creative work, which I have here termed "protoexistentialist," is characterized by progressive starvation and growing obsessions with astrology, psychopathology, and yes, metaphysics, conditioned partly, we may presume, by his quite rational desire to avoid conscription (he was a self-proclaimed pacifist), partly by his desperate attempts to retain a shred of hope and a sense of agency, and, in all likelihood, by the genuine deterioration of his mental state (he had obtained a diagnosis of schizophrenia). Thus, I feel justified in my placement of his NKVD confession letter (1931) at the beginning of this final phase, as it set into slow motion the execution of the existential nightmare of a decade lived under a suspended death sentence, which materialized only at the end of a decade of Stalinist repression.

ACKNOWLEDGMENTS

The transducer of these works wishes to gratefully acknowledge the invaluable support of the editors of the journals in which some of the essays, prose, and poems in this book first appeared: *Eleven Eleven, (ĕm): A Review of Text and Image, Gargoyle, Green Mountains Review, MAYDAY Magazine, Narrative, New American Writing, Numéro Cinq, Offcourse, PEN America, The International Literary Quarterly*, and *The Literary Review*. My thanks are also due to my editors at Northwestern University Press, Mike Levine and Anne Gendler, for his help in shaping my manuscript and her help in shaping this book. For her invaluable contribution in the latter stages of this work, I am forever indebted to my partner and sometimes cotranslator, the Russian American poet Dana Golin. And, of course, my gratitude to my parents, Elizabeth and Roman Cigale, in whose kitchen work on this book first began.

Russian Absurd

Selected Prose from the Early Years

✦ 1928–1933 ✦

From the Notebooks (1928)

July 26. I am altogether some sort of a special unfortunate. Hanging over me in recent times has been an incomprehensible law of "un-fulfillment." Whatever it is that I may wish for, it is precisely that which will not come true. Everything happens in a way contradictory to my expectations. Verily: man proposes and God disposes. I am terribly in need of money, and I will never have any, I know that! I know that in the nearest time, the most serious difficulties will befall me, that will make my whole life significantly worse than it has been up until now. From day to day, things are getting worse and worse. I no longer know what it is I should do. God's servant Ksenia, grant me your love, save me and guard over my entire family.

July 27. Who could advise me regarding what I should do? Esther* brings with her misfortune. I am being destroyed along with her. What must I do, either divorce her or . . . carry my cross? I was given the choice to avoid this, but I remained dissatisfied, and asked to be united with Esther. I was told yet again, do not be married! But despite "having caught a scare," I still insisted, I still tied my fate with Esther's, till death do us part. I myself was to blame for this or, rather, I did it to myself. What has happened to the OBERIU? Everything vanished as soon as Esther became a part of me. Since that time, I have ceased to write as I must and have only brought misfortune upon myself from all directions. Is it that I can't be dependent on women, no matter which one it is? Or is the nature of Esther's character such that she brought an end to my work? I don't know. If Esther is filled with sorrow, then how can I possibly let her go

* Daniil Kharms's first wife, Esther Rusakov (née Ioselevich), was repressed, along with her entire family, in 1936.

+ 5 +

away from me? And simultaneously, how can I permit my work, the OBERIU, to so completely collapse? Fate had attached me to Esther in response to my entreaties. And now I wish to break with fate a second time. Is this only a lesson or is it the end of the poet? If I am a poet, then fate will take pity on me and will once again lead me to greatness, making of me a free man. But perhaps the cross that I had called down upon myself will hang above me my entire life? And am I then right, as a poet, to remove it from myself? Where may I find counsel and resolution? Esther is as alien to me as the rational mind. In this, she is an impediment to me in everything, she irritates me. But I love her and only wish her well. It would be best for her to separate from me; I have no value for a rationalistic mind. Wouldn't she be better off without me? She could get married again and, perhaps, be luckier than she is with me. If she would only fall out of love with me to easier bear the separation! But is there anything I could do? How should I pursue a divorce? Lord, please help me! God's servant Ksenia, please help me! Make it so, that in the space of the next week, Esther leaves me and starts living happily. And so that I once again take up writing, being as free as before!

God's servant Ksenia, help us!

Daniil Kharms

I was sitting on the roof of the State Publishing House . . .

I was sitting on the roof of the State Publishing House and observing, to make sure that everything was going well, because as soon as you take your eye off things something bad will happen. You can't leave this city unattended for even a second. And who if not me to keep the city under a watchful eye? If anything untoward is happening, then we will immediately put a stop to it.

The rules for sentinels on the roof of the State Publishing House:

First Rule

The sentinel may be a man of the OBERIU faith, in possession of the traits listed below:

1. Of moderate height.
2. Brave.
3. Farsighted.
4. Voice booming and authoritative.
5. Mighty and without pretentions.
6. Able to make out by ear various sounds and not susceptible to boredom.
7. A smoker or, under extreme circumstances, a non-smoker.

Second Rule (What he must do)

1. The sentinel must sit at the very topmost point of the roof and, sparing no effort, diligently scan in all directions, for which

it is recommended to turn the head from left to right and vice versa, extending it in both directions to the limits of the vertebrae.

2. The sentinel must warrant that order in the city is observed, in such a way that:
   a. People not walk about willy-nilly, but as God himself had intended them to.
   b. That people ride around only in those coaches which are specifically designed for such a purpose.
   c. That people do not walk on roofs, cornices, pediments, and other similar points of high elevation.

Footnote: Permitted to carpenters, painters, and other manual laborers.

Third Rule (What the sentinel is not permitted to do)

1. To ride the roof's crest as though it were a horse.
2. To flirt with the ladies.
3. To insert his own words into the conversations of the people passing by.
4. To chase after sparrows or to adopt their habits.
5. To curse at policemen by calling them pharaohs.
6. (. . .)
7. To weep.

Fourth Rule (The sentinel's rights)

The sentinel has the right to:

1. Sing.
2. Shoot at whomever he will.
3. Invent and compose, and also take notes and read them aloud (not too loud), or memorize them.
4. Take in the panorama.
5. Compare the life below to an anthill.

6. Debate which books are published.
7. Bring with him bedsheets.

Fifth Rule

The sentinel is required to treat all firemen with utmost respect. *That is it.*

Founding members: Daniil Kharms
Boris Levin (signatures); Assisted by: Vladimirov (signature)

May 22, 1929

The Family Gibberundum

Once upon a time, a fly collided with the forehead of a gentleman running by and, passing through his head, exited out the back. The gentleman, by the name of Dernyatin,* was considerably perplexed: it seemed to him that something had whistled through his brain, and on the back of his head the skin popped and began to tickle. Dernyatin stopped and thought: "What could this possibly mean? For it is absolutely clear that I heard a whistling in my brain. Absolutely nothing comes now into my head that would help me understand what is going on in here. In any case, the sensation is quite rare, similar to some sort of a mental illness. But I won't think of this anymore and will continue my jog." With these thoughts in mind, Dernyatin ran along further. But no matter how far he ran, he couldn't reproduce the effect. On the deep blue path, Dernyatin misstepped and almost stumbled and even had to wave his arms around in the air to steady himself. "It is well I didn't fall," Dernyatin thought, "or I would've broken my glasses and would no longer be able to see where I was going." Dernyatin resumed walking, leaning on his walking stick. However, one danger followed upon another. Dernyatin started humming some sort of song, so as to dispel his dark thoughts. The song was a happy and mellifluous one, so that Dernyatin's attention was taken up with it and he forgot even that he was walking along a dark blue road, upon which this time of day, on most days, automobiles raced by at a dizzying pace. The dark blue road was especially narrow and it was quite difficult to jump aside from the path of an automobile. For this reason, it was considered

* Dernyatin is suggestive of *deorgat*, "to jerk," and *dryan'*, "trash."

a dangerous road. Vigilant people always walked on the blue road with great care so as not to get killed. Here, death awaited the pedestrian at every step, either in the form of a car or a dump truck, or in the form of a cart loaded with coal ore. Dernyatin didn't even have time to blow his nose before a giant automobile came hurtling his way. Dernyatin screamed, "I'm going to die!" and jumped aside. The grass parted before him and he fell into a wet ditch. The automobile flew by, thundering, raising above its roof the international flag of distress. The people in the automobile were certain that Dernyatin was dead, and had therefore removed their hats and proceeded hence bareheaded. "You didn't happen to notice which wheel the wayfarer fell under, under the front or the rear one?" asked a gentleman wearing a mufti, that is, not a mufti but a bashlyk. "My cheeks and the lobes of my ears are frostbitten," the gentleman was saying, "and so I am always wearing this bashlyk." Beside the gentleman, in the automobile sat a lady whose mouth gave her an interesting appearance. "I," the lady said, "am worried that we may be held accountable for the death of this wayfarer." "What? What?" asked the gentleman, pulling the bashlyk away from his ear. The lady repeated her concern. "No," the gentleman in the bashlyk said. "Manslaughter is prosecuted only in those instances when the victim resembles a pumpkin. And we are not. We are not. We are not culpable in the death of the wayfarer. He himself screamed, 'I am dying!' We were only the witnesses to his sudden demise." Madame Enet smiled with her interesting mouth and said under her breath, "Anton Antonich, you evade trouble quite adroitly." The gentleman Dernyatin lay in the damp ditch, his legs and arms splayed out. The automobile had already driven off. Dernyatin had already comprehended that he was not dead. Death, in the form of an automobile, had passed him over. He arose, brushed off his suit with his sleeve, spat on his fingers, and strode along the deep blue road to make up for lost time.

II

The Family Gibberundum lived in a little house by the slow-running river, Fierstream. Father Gibberundum, Platon Ilyich, loved all sorts of lore of high-flying fancy: Mathematics, Triordinate Philosophy, the Geography of Eden, the Collected Works of Screwycent, the Teachings of the Mortal Nudges, and the Celestial Hierarchy of Dionysus Aeropaginus were Platon Ilyich's most beloved subjects. The doors of the Gibberundum household were always open to all wayfarers who had undertaken pilgrimages to the sacred places of our planet. Tales of levitating hills, brought by various pilgrims from the Nikitinsky District, were met in the Gibberundum household with great excitement and intense interest. Platon Ilyich kept meticulous records of the details of the levitations of the major and minor hills. The takeoff of the Cabbaginsky Hill was particularly distinguished from that of all other takeoffs. As is well known, Cabbaginsky Hill alighted at night, at approximately 5:00, having uprooted and turned over a great cypress tree. From its takeoff point into the sky, the hill ascended not in an arc-shaped trajectory, like all other hills, but in a straight line, having performed slight perturbations only at an elevation of fifteen to sixteen kilometers. And the wind, blowing into the hillside, passed right through it, not even throwing it off its path. It was as though this hill of chartaceous origin had lost its property of impermeability. For example, a gull had transected the hill in its flight. It went right through it as though through a cloud. This observation was confirmed by several witnesses. And this contradicted all the known laws of levitating hills. But still, a fact remains a fact, and so Platon Ilyich entered it into the recorded data on the Cabbaginsky Hill. Each and every day at the Gibberundum house, honored guests would gather to deliberate on the features of the rules of alogical construction. Among these honored guests were the Professor of Railroads Mikhail Ivanovich Dumkopf, the Igumen Mulenos the Second, and the archecdysiast Stephan Dernyatin. The guests gathered in the first floor sitting room, seating themselves around an oblong table upon which was placed a commonplace trough, filled with water. The guests, engaged thus in conversation, spat in this trough: such was the custom in the Gibberundum household. Platon Ilyich himself sat holding in his hand a riding crop. From time to time, he would dunk it in the water and use it to lash the empty table. This was referred to as the "jostling of the tool" or "the jiggering of the instrument." At nine o'clock, Platon

Ilyich's wife, Anna Scriblerovna, would appear to lead the guests to the table. The guests consumed both solid and liquid victuals, and then would crawl toward Anna Scriblerovna on their knees, kiss her dainty hand, and sit down to drink tea. At tea, the Igumen Mulenos the Second told of an occurrence that had happened to him fourteen years previous. He claimed that he, as a novitiate, was sitting on the stoop of his porch feeding the ducks. All of a sudden, a fly zoomed out of the house, buzzed around and around, and slammed into the igumen's forehead. It slammed into his forehead, flew through his head, and exiting out the back, flew back into the house. The igumen remained sitting on the porch with an exalted smile, in amazement that he had, with his own two eyes, finally witnessed a miracle. The other guests, having heard Mulenos the Second out, slapped themselves with spoons across their lips and their Adam's apples as a sign that the evening had drawn to its conclusion. Afterward, the evening began to assume a frivolous character. Anna Scriblerovna left the room, and the gentleman archecdysiast Dernyatin sounded forth on the theme of "women and flowers." On occasion, some of the guests would stay overnight. Then, several drawers would be slid together and they would serve as a bed for Mulenos the Second. Professor Dumkopf would sleep in the dining room on the grand piano, and the gentleman Dernyatin got in bed with the Gibberundum maid, Masha. But on most occasions, the guests left for their own houses. Platon Ilyich locked the doors behind them himself and went off to Anna Scriblerovna's. On the river Fierstream, the Nikitinsky fishermen could be heard floating down, singing their songs. And the family Gibberundum would fall asleep to the songs of the boatmen.

III

Platon Ilyich Gibberundum became stuck in the doorway of his dining room. He sunk his elbows into the doorframes, his feet became rooted in the wooden threshold, he rolled out his eyes, and he stood there, frozen.

[*1929–30*]

The Saber

§1

Life is divided into working time and non-working time. Non-working time creates structures—pipes. Working time fills these pipes.

Work in the form of wind flies into a bass pipe. The pipe sings in a lazy voice. We listen to the wailing of the pipes. And our bodies suddenly grow light and stream into a beautiful wind; we suddenly become a reflection of ourselves: to the right a little hand, to the left a little hand, to the right a little foot, to the left a little foot; our sides and ears and eyes and shoulders are our boundaries with the rest. Just as rhymes do, our edges shimmer like a steel blade.

§2

Non-working time is an empty pipe. In our non-working time, we lie on the couch, smoke and drink a lot, visit friends, talk a lot, apologize before each other. We justify our actions, separating them, as it were, from everything else, and say that we are right to exist independently. That is when it begins to seem to us that we possess everything that is outside of us. And everything that exists outside of ourselves and is separate from us and from everything else, distinguishable from us and from its (that of which we are now speaking) environment (even if only filled with empty air), we term the object. The object is set apart by us as an independent world and begins to possess everything that lies outside it, just as we possess all the same.

Independently existing objects are no longer bound by the laws of logical sets and they bound about in space wherever they will, at will, just as we. Nouns* give birth to verbs and bestow onto verbs independent choice. Objects, in the wake of nouns, complete various actions, as free as the new verb. New qualities arise, and in their wake also free adjectives. In this way develops a new generation of parts of speech. Speech, liberated from logic's course, runs along novel paths, disarticulated from other kinds of speech. The edges of speech shine a bit brighter, so that we are able to see where is the end and where the beginning, otherwise we would become entirely lost. These edges, these breezes, fly into the empty verse-pipe. The pipe begins to hum and we hear the rhyme.

§3

Yeah! verses have outpaced us
We are unfree just like the verse.
In pipes' winds harmony is heard,
We are weakened and made terse.
Where are the limits of our torsos,
Where are our shimmering flanks?
We are hazy just like tulle,
We are helpless as a rule.
Words and speeches on the wind,
And objects galloping after them,
And we are fighting in the breach—
Glory be, we scream, to victories!

In such a way, we become immersed in the working condition. Then, there is no time for thinking about food or guests. Conversations cease to justify our deeds. During a fight, one does not justify oneself or apologize. Now, everyone is responsible for oneself alone. By his own volition alone he puts himself in motion and passes through

* The literal meaning of Russian *sushchestvitel'nye* is "existing words."

the others. Everything existing outside of ourselves has ceased to be in ourselves. We no longer resemble the world that surrounds us. The world is flying into our mouths in the guise of separate little particles: made of stone, pitch tar, glass, iron, wood, etc. Approaching the table we say: This is a table, and not me, and therefore, here you go!—and, thwack, on the table with the side of the fist, and the table splits in half, and the halves crumble into powder, and we stomp the powder, and the powder flies into our mouths, and we say: this is dust, and not me—and we take a swipe at the dust. But the dust no longer feels any fear of our fists.

§4

We stand here and say: Now I have stretched one hand out directly in front of me, and the other hand back. And in the front, I end where the tip of my hand is, and behind me I also end there, where my hand ends. Above, I end at the top of my head, below at my heels, to the sides at my shoulders. And that is all of me. And what is outside of me, that is no longer me.

Now that we have become entirely self-sufficient, let us wipe clean our edges, that we gain better knowledge of where what is no longer us begins. Let us wipe clean our nethermost—boots; our uppermost—the tops of our heads, which we will designate with a little hat; we will decorate our hands with the most resplendent cuffs, and on our shoulders we will wear epaulets. And now, it is absolutely clear for all to see, where we end and where all the rest begins.

§5

Here are three of our pairs of edges:

1. hand—hand.
2. shoulder—shoulder.
3. back of the head—heels.

Question: Has our work begun? And if it has begun, what does it consist in?

Answer: Our work is about to begin, and it consists in registering the world, for we are no longer the world.

Question: If we are no longer of the world then what are we?

Answer: No, we are of the world. That is, I did not express myself quite precisely. It is not as though we are not of the world, but that we are separate unto ourselves, and it is separate unto itself. I will now clarify this: There exist numbers: 1, 2, 3, 4, 5, 6, 7, etc. All these numbers make up the numerical or counting order. Every number will find in it its place. But 1—is a special number. It may stand off by itself to one side, as an indicator of the absence of a count. 2 is already the first multiplicity, and beyond 2 so all the other numbers. Some savages know how to count only in this way: once and many. And so are we in the world, like the one in the counting order.

Question: Good, but how are we to go about registering the world?

Answer: Just as the one registers all the other numbers, i.e., by fitting inside them and seeing what happens as a result.

Question: Does the single unit register thus the other numbers?

Answer: Let's assume that this is the case. This is unimportant.

Question: Strange. Then how are we to fit ourselves into the other objects, distributed in the world? By observing how much longer, wider, and taller the wardrobe is than we? Like so, is it?

Answer: The one is symbolized by us as the sign with the appearance of a stick. This icon for one is only the most convenient one for symbolizing the one, as is every other sign for a number. Just so we ourselves are but the most convenient form of ourselves.

The one, in registering the two, does not with its sign correspondingly fit within the sign of the two. The one registers numbers through its quality. And that is how we must act.

Question: But what is the meaning of our quality?

Answer: The death of the ear is hearing,
the death of the nose is nausea,
the death of the sky is silence,
the death of the eye—blindness.

We also know the abstract quality of this singularity. But this understanding exists in us as an understanding of something. Let's say, a fathom. The one registers the two—there is this: one fathom fits within two fathoms, one match fits within two matches, and so forth. There are many such singularities. Just so man is not one, but many. And we have just as many qualities as there are people in existence. And each of us possesses our own particular quality.

Question: What quality do I possess?

Answer: Yes. The work begins with a search for our particular quality. Because we will need to later arm ourselves with this quality, let us call it an armament.

Question: But how am I to find my armament?

§7

If there no longer be the means
To defeat the march of reason,
Let's leave the battlefield with pride
And go on with our peaceful ride.
A peaceful ride is building a house
Out of logs with the use of an ax.
I enter the world deafened by thunder,
The houses multiplied to a mountain.
But the saber's a remnant of war,
And my only remaining solid form.
Blaring, it chops from swallows' roofs
The logs I have no strength to scoop;
Should I be changing arts or arms?

Chop down enemies or raise a house?
Strip bark from oak like a virgin's lace,
Then stick the saber in her heart?
I'm a carpenter armed with a saber,
I duel the house as though my foe.
The house of sabers at defeat's center
Stands lowering its horns to the ground.
Here is my saber, it's my full measure—
My fate, my quill feather, my Megaera!

The Afterword.

§8

Kozma Prutkov registered the world as a testing chamber and therefore he was armed with a saber.

In possession of a saber were: Goethe, Blake, Lomonosov, Gogol, Prutkov, and Khlebnikov. Having armed oneself with a saber, one may proceed to the business at hand of registering the world.

§9

The registration of the world
(The saber—is our measure)
that's all

November 19–20, 1929

A tramcar was running along the tracks . . .

A tramcar was running along the tracks. Invisible in the glare of its two headlights was a toad. The tram contains every convenience for sitting and for standing. May its tail, and the people sitting in it, not be held accountable, and the people walking toward the exit also. Among them, we will find animals of an entirely different order. There are also the males of the species for whom there was no room in the car, and they are now scrambling to get onto another car. May as well let them all go to hell! The thing is that this was in the midst of a driving rain, so that it was not immediately possible to tell whether it was water or a traveler that was running down the sidewalk. Let us analyze this step by step, according to the facts. If one stands outside in a suit jacket then, in a very short time, it will soak through and stick to your body—therefore, it was driving rain. But if one were to yell out: Who goes there?—then a window on the first floor would open, and a head stick out, belonging to whomever, only not to a human being, who had seen the truth, that water refreshes and dignifies the features of a face—and it would reply menacingly: See this (simultaneously, in the window appears something resembling both a cavalryman's boot and an ax)? I'll let you have it twice, so that you get it quick! Judging by this, a traveler was running, and if not in this case exactly a vagabond, then anyway such a one as can be found somewhere nearby, perhaps even within the confines of that window.

[*1930*]

We lay on the bed . . .

I

We lay on the bed. She lay facing the wall with the cupboards, and I lay facing the side table. Only four words could be said about me: his ears stick out. She knew it all.

II

Is it a fork? Or an angel? Or one hundred rubles? It's Nola. The fork's too small. The angel's tallish. The money ran out a long time ago. And Nola—that's her. She's one lone Nola. There were once six Nolas, and she's one of them.

III

A doggy wearing a little hat approached us. Its steps were swimming resoundingly. A fly opened the window. Come on, let's look out the window!

IV

We can't see nuthin' out the window. Can you see anything? I can't see nuthin', and you? I see skis. So who's on the skis? A soldier's on the skis, and he's got a belt slung over his shoulder, but he himself is beltless.

[*1930*]

Let us look out of the window . . .

Let us look out of the window: there, in both directions, we will see rails receding into the distance. Seated in the tramcars are people counting how many feet they have ridden on their fingers, for their fares are determined by the foot. Now let us look into a scope: here we will note a smallish flatbread, now lighted, now dark. Gentlemen, this is not a flatbread but a sphere.

At this point in time, on a flat board stood three objects: a pitcher, a bolide, and a human being wearing a blue tie.

The pitcher said: Gentlemen, let us look upon the merman earth.

Where? the bolide thundered.

Upon that sphere which is visible in the scope, said the pitcher. That sphere is the earth.

Human being: I am an inhabitant of the earth.

Bolide: I am an inhabitant of the vast space.

Pitcher: I am an inhabitant of Eden.

All three grew silent and past them walked not a living thing, and no one rode, and no one flew by.

The pitcher said:

Oh, Hu! Oh Hum! Oh Humhu! Tell me how they live among you. What do they do?

The human said, opening his mouth:

I am a human from earth. You all know this. I am not a merman. I am the merman's neighbor—a Russian. My name is Grigoriev. If you'd like, I will tell you everything.

Out of the water emerged three swarthy men and yelled, stomping their feet:

Please!

The human being began:

So I go to the food cooperative and say: Give me that can of sardines over there. And they tell me: We have no sardines, these cans are empty. And I tell them: Why are you pulling my leg? And they tell me: It's not our idea. So whose idea is it? It's due to the shortages, because the Kyrgyz have rustled away all the split-hoofed ungulates. So are there any vegetables? I ask them. No vegetables either. All bought up. Keep quiet, Grigoriev.

And the human being finished with a song:

I, Grigoriev, just shut up,
And began to carry binocs.
I look through them and look,
And see the stacks to come.

The End

[*1930*]

Beaverson was walking down the road . . .

Beaverson was walking down the road pondering: why is it that when you pour sand in the soup, its taste becomes spoiled?

All of a sudden, he saw a tiny little girl sitting in the road, holding in her hands a worm and crying loudly.

What are you crying about? Beaverson asked the little girl.

I'm not crying, said the little girl, I am singing.

Then why are you singing like that? asked Beaverson.

To make the worm happy, the girl said, and they call me Natasha.

So that's how it is? Beaverson said, taken aback.

Yes, that's how it is, said the girl. Good-bye. And the girl hopped up, climbed on a bicycle, and pedaled away.

So small and already riding bicycles, Beaverson thought to himself.

[*1930*]

Theme for a Story

A certain engineer sets before himself the task of building a huge brick wall across all of Petersburg. He ponders how this may be done, and stays up all night mulling over it. Gradually, a circle of thinker-engineers forms and develops a plan for building the wall. It is decided to build the wall at night, and in such a way that it is all built in a single night, so that it appears as a surprise. The workers are called together. Assignments are handed out. The civic authorities are distracted, and finally the night arrives upon which the wall is to be built. Only four people are aware of the plan to build the wall. The construction workers and the engineers receive precise assignments, where it is they should stand and what they should do. Thanks to such exact planning, they succeed in building the wall in a single night. On the next day Petersburg is all topsy-turvy. And the inventor himself is feeling in the dumps. How this wall should be used didn't occur to him either.

[*1929–30*]

The Whorld

I told myself that I see the world. But the whole world was inaccessible to my gaze, and I saw only parts of it. And all that I saw, I called parts of the world. And I observed the qualities of these parts and, in observing the qualities of the parts, I was doing science. I understood that there were intelligent qualities of parts and unintelligent qualities in those very same parts. And so I divided them and I gave them names. And in accordance with these qualities, the parts of the world were either intelligent or unintelligent.

And there were such parts of the world that were capable of thought. And these parts looked at the other parts, and they looked at me. And all the parts resembled each other, and I resembled them.

> And I said: Parts are thunder.
> The parts replied: Farts of time.
> I said: I'm also part of three turns.
> Parts averred: But we're only small points.

And suddenly I ceased to see them, and then the other parts as well. And I was afraid the world would end.

But then I understood that I do not see the parts individually, but all at once. First I thought that this was NOTHING. But then I understood that this is the world, and that which I saw before was not the world.

And I always knew what the world was, but that which I saw before, I do not know even now.

And when the parts vanished, then their intelligent qualities ceased to be intelligent, and their unintelligent qualities ceased to be unintelligent. And the world ceased being intelligent and unintelligent.

But as soon as I understood that I saw the world, I ceased to see it. And I was afraid, thinking the world had ended. But as long as I thought so, I understood that, had the world indeed vanished, then I would no longer be thinking this. And I looked out, seeking the world, but found it not.

And then there was no longer anywhere left to look.

That is when I understood that as long as there was somewhere to look, around me was the world. And now it is no longer. There is only me.

> But the world is not me.
> Though, at the same time,
> I am the world.
> But the world isn't me.
> But I am the world.
> But the world isn't me.
> But I am the world.
> But the world isn't me.
> But I am the world.
> And then I thought no more.

May 30, 1930

I want to tell you about a series of events . . .

I want to tell you about a series of events that happened to a fish or, more precisely, not to a fish but to a man named Gardesman [Patrulev] and, even more precisely, not even to Gardesman himself but to his daughter.

I'll begin with her birth. By the way, regarding births: on our floor were born . . . Perhaps it's best I tell you this part later.

OK, so I'll tell it to you straight:

Gardesman's daughter was born on a Saturday. We'll designate this daughter with the Latin letter M.

Having designated this daughter with the Latin letter M, we may note that:

1. Two hands, two feet, 'n' in between, her boots.
2. The ears may be as capable as the eyes.
3. To run—is a run-of-the-mill verb.
4. To finger—is a verb at hand.
5. A mustache must ache.
6. One can't use the back of one's head to tell what's hanging on the wall.
17. Take note that the number six is followed immediately by the number seventeen.

So that we may form an exact picture, let us memorize these seventeen postulates.

Now, leaning with our hand on the fifth postulate, let us see what may come of it.

If we were to lean against the fifth postulate with a donkey cart or with sugar or with a natural string, then we would be forced to say: yes, indeed, and something else besides.

Let's see what we have now.

You look over here, and I will look over here, so that, as a result, we are both looking over there.

Or, speaking more precisely, I'm looking over there, and you're looking in another place.

Let us now determine for ourselves what it is that we see. For this purpose, it is sufficient to clarify separately what it is I see and what it is you see.

I see one half of the house, and you see the other half of the town. For simplicity's sake, let us call this a wedding.

Let us now consider Gardesman's daughter. Her wedding took place, let us say, at about this time. If the wedding had been held earlier, we would have said that the wedding had been held before its time. If the wedding had been held later, then we would have said "Wave," because the wedding would have been held later.

All the seventeen postulates or so-called feathers are self-evident. We may now proceed further.

> The following is thicker than the preceding
> A catfish is thicker than an oil lamp
> A moray eel is thicker than a scallion
> A book is thicker than a notebook
> but all notebooks are thicker than one notebook
> This here table is thicker than a book
> This conclusion is thicker than the floor
> This table is thicker than the previous one
> and the previous one taller than a scallion
> A scallion of course smaller than a comb
> just as a hat is smaller than a daybed
> that is large enough to fit
> a box filled with books
> but the box
> is deeper than a hat
> the hat softer
> more silken than a ship propeller
> however a bee is spicier than a ball.
> Exactly as beautiful

is that which grows on this side
and on that side of the fence.
Still a book is more elastic than soup
the ear more flexible than a book.
Soup is more jellied and fatter than a scallion
and heavier than a key.

Confirming statements:

The rabbit has arms instead of mustaches.
On the back of Father's head is a pheasant.
The store has four buttons.
The long-horned beetle has a dandelion.
The sword has a sash.
The newspaper has eight medallions.
I have a tail.
You, a rocking cradle.
Giants wear a hat.

Conjunctions:

The house with a beak.
A toddleroo with a Tatar.
A caravel constructor in kerosene.
A plate without any hair.
A crow between inconspicuous dates.
A fur coat with a crack named Fofa.
Dalya in dire straits.
A Romanian from the handwashing stand.
The angel of perches.

Digressions:

The cock was escaping the water.
Jean was escaping his beard.
The nail was escaping the paraffin.
The little whip jumped out of the vase.

The sable was escaping the cockroach.
Experience sliding from under the glass.
The astronomer escaping a wad of cotton.
The key was lying elongated.

Correlations.

The house with a beak.
A toddleroo with a Tatar.
A caravel constructor in kerosene.
A plate without any hair.
A crow between inconspicuous dates.
A fur coat with a crack named Fofa.
Dalya in dire straits.
A Romanian from the handwashing stand.
The angel named Perches.

Discussion.

This isn't a smithy but a pail.
This isn't rice but a ruler.
This isn't a glove but the warehouse superintendent.
This isn't an eye but a knee.
It isn't I who came here but you.
This isn't water but tea.
This isn't a nail but a screw.
Fur not light.
A man with one hand not a room with one window.
These are shoes not nails.
These are shoes not kidneys.
Exactly the same and not nostrils.

Conclusions.

Gardesman the father's daughter is Gardesman's daughter.
Which also means that the father's daughter is his daughter.
If so then it means the daughter of Gardesman the father

is also Gardesman the father's daughter.
So there's the daughter and father Gardesman.
Gardesman's daughter and father Gardesman.
Which means Gardesman's daughter's father is Gardesman.
And no one could possibly ever say he is Cockerman.
    That would be self-contradictory.

[1930]

Once upon a time Andrey Vasilievich . . .

1

Once upon a time Andrey Vasilievich was walking down the street and lost his watch. Soon after, he died. His father, a hunchbacked old man, sat up all night in a cylinder hat clenching in his left hand a cane with a crooked handle. All sorts of thoughts raced through his head, among them that life is a smithy's workshop.

2

Andrey Vasilievich's father, Gregory Antonovich, or rather Vasily Antonovich, embraced Maria Mikhailovna and called her his royal majesty. She, silently and with fervent hope, gazed straight ahead and up above. And that's when that scoundrel of a hunchback, Vasily Antonovich, decided to annihilate his hump.

3

For this purpose, Vasily Antonovich got in his saddle and rode over to Professor Mamaev's. Professor Mamaev was sitting in the garden reading a book. In response to all of Vasily Antonich's entreaties, Mamaev replied with but a single word: "Soon enough." That's when Vasily Antonovich went and checked himself into the surgical ward.

4

The doctor's assistants and the sisters of mercy helped Vasily Antonovich onto the table and covered him with a sheet. Then Professor Mamaev entered the room himself. "Would you like a shave?" the professor asked. "No. Please remove my hump," said Vasily Antonovich.

The operation began. But it ended in failure, because one of the sister-nurses covered her face with a plaid rag and could not see a thing, and so could not assist in handing over the necessary instruments. And the doctor's assistant covered his mouth and nose so that he couldn't breathe and toward the end of the operation he gagged and dropped dead to the floor. But the most unpleasant thing was that Professor Mamaev, because he was rushing, forgot to remove from the patient the sheet and instead of the hump resected something else. The back of his head I think. And the hump he only probed and poked at with the surgical scissors.

5

Returning home, Vasily Antonovich could not calm down until some Spaniards forced their way into the house and chopped off the back of the cook Andryusha's head.

6

Having calmed down, Vasily Antonovich went to see another doctor who, in very short order, cut off his hump.

7

Then everything proceeded splendidly. Maria Mikhailovna divorced Vasily Antonovich and married Bubnov.

8

Bubnov did not love his new wife. As soon as she would leave the house, Bubnov would buy himself a new hat and incessantly greet his neighbor, Anna Moiseevna. However, suddenly, one of Anna Moiseevna's teeth broke and, out of pain, she opened her mouth wide open. Bubnov began to take pains to ponder over his biography.

9

Bubnov's father, by the name of Snort, fell in love with Bubnov's mother, by the name of Oink. Once, Oink sat on her stove collecting mushrooms that were growing nearby. But Snort unexpectedly said this—Oink, I want Bubnov to be born to us.

Oink asked:

—Bubnov? I see, I see.

—Precisely so, Your Majesty answered Snort.

10

Oink and Snort sat next to each other and began to think of all the many funny things and they laughed and laughed.

11

And so Oink finally gave birth to Bubnov.

[*second half of March 1931*]

The Power of Words

The power that words are invested with must be liberated. There are such combinations of words that make the effect of this power more evident. We must not think that this power is capable of moving objects. But I am certain that it is capable of this also. And the most valuable effect of this force is almost inexpressible. We obtain a crude understanding of it from the rhythmic effect of metrical verses. Those complex means, such as the assistance that metrical verses receive from the motion of one or another part of the body, we also must not consider to be a figment of the imagination. This is the crudest but at the same time the most subtle manifestation of the power of language. It is likely that the more involved action of this force is not subject to our conscious understanding. If it were possible to consider the method of investigating these effects, then such a method must be entirely dissimilar from the methods utilized heretofore by science. In this, first and foremost, is that neither fact nor experience may serve as proof. I am at a loss to say what might serve to prove and verify what I have said here. Up to this point in time, I am aware of only four types of verbal mechanisms: verses, prayers, songs, and spells. These mechanisms are constructed not according to the track of calculation or reasoning, but in an entirely different way, that goes by the name of the ALPHABET.

May 1931

How strange it is . . .

How strange it is, how inexpressibly strange, that behind this wall, behind this very wall, a man is sitting on the floor, stretching out his long legs in orange boots, an expression of malice on his face.

We need only drill a hole in the wall and look through it and immediately we would see this mean-spirited man sitting there.

But we shouldn't think about him. What is he anyway? Is he not after all a portion of death in life, materialized out of our own conception of emptiness? Whoever he may be, God bless him.

June 22, 1931

Morning

Yes, today I had a dream about a dog.

It was licking a rock, and then it trotted down to the river and proceeded to look into the water.

Did it see something in there?

What was it that it glimpsed in the water?

I lit a cigarette. There were only two left.

Once I smoke these, I will have none left.

No money, either.

Where will I eat dinner today?

In the morning I can have some tea. I still have sugar left and a bun. But there will be no cigarettes. And no place to eat dinner.

I should get up soon. It's already half past two.

I lit a second cigarette and started thinking, how can I manage to eat dinner today.

Foma has dinner at the Publishing Union at seven. If I arrive at the House of Print precisely at seven, I could meet Foma there and tell him: "Listen, Foma Antonovich, I would like you to feed me dinner today. I was supposed to be paid today, but the credit union didn't have any money." Or I could borrow a ten from the professor. But the professor will likely say, "Forgive me. I owe you money and you are borrowing money from me. But I don't have a ten now. I can only give you three." Or the professor will say, "I don't have a kopek left." Or no, the professor will say not that but this: "Here's a ruble, and I'll give you nothing more. Go and buy yourself a box of matches."

I finished the cigarette and began to get dressed.

Volodya called. Tatyana Alexandrovna said about me that she can't understand what in me is divine and what foolish.

I put on my boots. The heel of the right one is coming off.

Today is Sunday.

I am walking along Liteyny Prospect past the bookstores. Only yesterday, I was asking for a miracle.

Yes, yes, if only a miracle occured right now.

A half-snow, half-rain begins to fall. I stop in front of the bookstore and look at the window display. I read ten book titles and immediately forget them.

I reach into my pocket for cigarettes but remember I have none left.

I make a screwed-up face and quickly walk off toward Nevsky Prospect, tapping with my walking stick. The house on the corner of Nevsky is being painted a disgusting yellow color. I am forced to walk around it in the street and am elbowed by the passersby. All of them have only recently arrived from the countryside and don't know how to use the sidewalk. It is very difficult to distinguish their filthy suits and faces from one another.

They trample in all directions, growl and shove.

Having accidentally bumped into one another, they don't say "excuse me" but shout out rude words at each other.

On the Nevsky Prospect sidewalk, there is a terrible jostle. The street itself is reasonably peaceful. Occasionally, trucks and private automobiles fly by.

The trolleys pass by filled to their gills. People hang off on their steps. Inside the tram, there is a perpetual grumbling. Everybody tells everyone else off: "You . . . !" When the doors swing open, a warm and stinking air wafts from inside the car onto the stairwell. People jump on and off without waiting for the tram to come to a stop. But they haven't yet learned to do it well, and so they hop up and down, forward and backward. Quite often, someone falls off and, with a howl and cursing, slips under the tram wheels. The policemen blow their whistles, stop the wagon cars, and fine the ones jumping on the move. But as soon as the tram moves again, new people run up and jump on it, grabbing the handlebars with their left hands.

Today I woke up at two o'clock.

I lay in bed till three without the energy to get up. I was pondering my dream. Why was the dog looking into the river and what did it see there? I assured myself that this is of great importance, to interpret the dream conclusively. But I couldn't remember what I saw in the dream after this and so I began thinking of something else.

Last night I sat at the table and smoked a lot. Some paper lay before me so that I might write something. But I didn't know what it was I was supposed to write. I didn't even know if this should be verses or a story or my thoughts. I wrote nothing and lay down to sleep. But I didn't sleep for very long. I wanted to know what I was supposed to write. I listed in my head all the types of literary expression, but didn't recognize my type. It could have been one word, or perhaps I was supposed to write an entire book. I asked God for a miracle, and started to crave a smoke. I had only four cigarettes left. It would be good to leave at least two, no three, for the morning.

I sat up on the bed and lit a cigarette.

I was asking God for some sort of miracle.

I lit the lamp and looked around. Nothing had changed.

And nothing was supposed to have changed in my room.

Something should have changed in me.

I looked up at the clock. Seven past three. That means I had to sleep no later than eleven thirty. I must fall asleep!

I extinguished the lamp and lay down.

No, I should lie on my left side.

I lay down on my left side and started to drift off.

I look out the window and see the street cleaner sweeping the street.

I stand beside the street sweeper and tell him that, before one is able to write something, one must know the words one ought to write.

A flea is hopping down my leg.

I lie with my face in the pillow with my eyes closed and try to sleep. But I hear the flea is jumping and look for it. If I move, sleep will escape me.

But here I must raise my hand and touch my forehead with a finger. I raise my hand and touch my forehead with my finger.

And the dream has vanished.

I want to turn onto my right side, but I must lie on my left.

Now the flea is on my back. It will bite me any second.

I say, ouch, ouch.

With my eyes closed, I see how the flea hops down my bedsheet, climbs into a fold, and sits there calmly, like a little dog.

I can see my entire room, but not from the side or from above, but together all at once. All the objects in it are orange.

I cannot fall asleep. I try not to think of anything. I remember that this is impossible and try not to strain my thoughts. Let them think what they may. Then I'm thinking of a giant spoon and recall a fable about a Tatar who saw in his dream a fruit compote but forgot to bring a spoon into the dream. And then he saw a spoon but forgot . . . forgot . . . forgot. That is, I forgot what I was thinking about. Could I be dreaming? I open my eyes to check.

Now I'm awake. How sad, because I was already falling asleep and forgot that I even needed to sleep. I must try again to fall asleep. How many efforts have evaporated into nothing? I yawned.

I was now too lazy to fall asleep.

I see the oven before me. In the dark, it looks dark green. I close my eyes but continue to see the oven. It is completely dark green. And all the objects are dark green. My eyes are closed, but I am able to blink without opening them.

A person continues to blink with eyes closed—I think—only a sleeper does not blink.

I see my room and I see myself, lying on the bed. I'm covered with a blanket, almost head to foot. Only my face barely peeks out.

In the room, all is a gray tone.

This is not a color but only its essence. Objects are prepared for colors. But the colors are stripped. Even though this tablecloth is gray, you can tell that in reality it is blue. And though this pencil is gray, in reality it is yellow.

I hear a voice—Asleep.

Oct. 25, 1931, Sunday

Is It Possible to Reach the Moon
by Throwing a Stone?

It was a terribly dark night. Although the stars gave off a glimmer, they did not shine. It was impossible to see a thing. Perhaps there was a tree standing nearby, but maybe it was a lion, or maybe an elephant, and maybe there was just nothing there. But then the moon rose and it became light out. It was possible then to make out a cliff and in the cliff a cave, and a meadow to the left, and to the right a stream, and beyond the stream a forest.

Out of the cave emerged, on all fours, two apes, and then they stood up, on their hind legs, and set off with an unsteady gait, their long arms swinging.

[*1931*]

Here I am sitting on a stool . . .

Here I am sitting on a stool. And the stool stands on the floor. And the floor is part of the house. And the house stands on the ground. And the ground extends in all directions, to the right and to the left, forward and backward. Is there an end to it anywhere?

It isn't possible that it doesn't end somewhere! It must end at some point or other! And then what? Water? And the ground floats on water? That's what people used to think. And they thought that there, where the water ends, is where the water and the sky meet.

And indeed, if you stand on a steamship at sea, where all around nothing interrupts your vision, then that is how it seems, that somewhere very far away the sky descends and unites with the water.

And the sky appeared to people as a big solid cupola, made of something transparent, like glass. But that was before anyone knew about glass and they said the sky is made of crystal. And they called the sky firmament. And people thought the sky or firmament is the most solid thing there is, the most consistent. Everything may change, but the firmament will never change. And to this day, when we wish to say of something, that it will not change, we say: this has been confirmed.

And people saw how the sun and the moon move across the sky, but the stars stand immobile. People began to pay closer attention to the stars and they noticed that the stars are distributed in the sky in the shape of figures. Here are seven stars placed in the form of a pot with a handle, here are three stars one following right upon another as though on a ruler. People learned to distinguish one star from another and they determined that the stars are also in motion, only all together, as though they are fixed to the sky and they move together with the sky itself. And people decided that the sky circles around the earth.

And then people divided the entire sky into distinct figures consisting of stars and each figure they called a constellation and each constellation they gave its own name.

And then people saw that not all stars move together with the sky but that there are some which wander among the other stars. And they called these stars planets.

[*1931*]

At two o'clock past midday
on Nevsky Prospect . . .

At two o'clock past midday on Nevsky Prospect or, more precisely, on the Prospect of the 25th of October,* nothing in particular happened. No, no, that man standing by the Coliseum store stopped there purely by accident. Perhaps the shoelaces of his boots came untied, or maybe he stopped to light a cigarette. Or no, not that at all! He's simply new in town and doesn't know the way. But where then are his things? Well no, wait, now he is lifting his head up, as though wishing to look up at the third floor, or even the fourth floor, even the fifth. No, look again, he only sneezed and is now walking on. He is a bit hunched and holds his shoulders hiked up. His green greatcoat is blowing open in the wind. And now he has just turned off onto Nadezhinskaya and disappeared behind a corner.

A man of Eastern extraction, a boot polisher, looks up in his wake and with his hand brushes smooth his luxurious black mustaches.

His coat is long, tight-fitting, and lilac in color, either checkered or, perhaps, striped in pattern, or is it, the devil take it! all in polka dots.

[*1931*]

* 25th of October, aka "The October Revolution."

Before I enter, I will knock . . .

Before I enter, I will knock on your window. You will see me in the window. Then I will walk through the door and you will see me in the doorway. Then I will walk into your house and you will recognize me. And I will enter you, and no one, except you, will see me and recognize me.

You will see me in the window.

You will see me in the doorway.

[*1931*]

Numbers cannot be defined
by their sequence . . .

Numbers cannot be defined by their sequence. Each number does not presuppose itself to be in the vicinity of other numbers. We differentiate between the arithmetic and the natural, interconnected orders of numbers. An arithmetic sum gives us a new number, the natural relating of numbers does not. There is no such thing as equivalence in nature. There is homogeneity, correlation, representation, distinction, and juxtaposition.

Nature does not equate one thing with another. Two trees can never be equal to one another. They can be equal in their lengths, their widths, in their qualities more generally. But two trees, in the totality of their nature, may never be the equals of one another. Many people think that numbers are comprehended quantities extracted from nature. We think that numbers are an order of reality. We believe that numbers are similar in essence to trees or grasses. But whereas trees may be subjected to the action of time, numbers are at all times unalterable. Time and space have no effect on numbers. This permanence of numbers is what allows them to be the measure of all things.

When we say "two," we do not mean that it is one plus another one. When, above, we said "two trees," then we had used only one of the properties of "two" and closed our eyes to all its other qualities. "Two trees" meant that we were talking of one tree and of yet another tree. In this instance, the word "two" expressed only the quantity as placed within the numerical order or, as we conceive it, within the counting wheel, between the numbers one and three. The counting wheel has a motion whose origin is entirely its own. It emerges out of the linear figure called the cross.

[*1932?*]

The infinite: that is the answer to all questions . . .

The infinite: that is the answer to all questions. All questions have but a single answer. Therefore, there is not a multiplicity of questions, there is only one question. This question is: "What is infinity?" I wrote this down on a piece of paper, reread it, and continued writing: "Infinity, it seems to us, has a direction, because we are accustomed to perceiving things visually. Largeness corresponds to a long segment, and smallness to a short segment. Infinity is a straight line that has no end, either to the right or to the left. But such a straight line is inaccessible to our understanding. If a smooth, flat object lies on a perfectly smooth floor, then we are able to grasp such an object only if we are able to touch its edges; we would then be able to pry under the edge of such an object and thus pick it up. One cannot pry under an infinite line; we cannot grasp it with our thoughts. It doesn't intersect with us anywhere; for anything to be intersected, its end, which does not exist, must be discovered. This is the point tangent to the circle of our thoughts. Its point of contact is so immaterial, so minute, that essentially, no such contact exists. It is represented by a point. And a point is an infinitely nonexistent figure. That is why we imagine a point as an infinitely tiny dot. But this is a false point. And our perception of an infinite line is likewise false. The infinity of two directions is so incomprehensible that it doesn't even concern us, doesn't seem strange to us, and moreover, it doesn't even exist for us. But the infinity of one direction, one having a beginning, now that infinity is stunning to us. It pierces us either with its beginning or its end, and the segment of the infinite line that creates a cord in the circle of our consciousness is, on the one hand, grasped by us, on the other hand it connects us with the eternal. To imagine to oneself that something never had a beginning and will never end is something we can do only in a distorted way. This perspective is: something never had a beginning and therefore it will never end. This idea about something is an idea about nothing at all. We make a connection between the beginning and the ending and from this deduce the first theorem: that which has no point of beginning has no point where it will end, and that which has a point where it begins has a place where it ends. The first is infinity, the second is finite. The first is nothing, the second—something."

I wrote all of this down, reread it, and started to think in this way:

"We are not aware of a phenomenon that is single in direction. If there is a motion to the right, then there must be a motion to the left as well. If there is a direction upwards, then it presupposes within itself the existence of a direction downwards. This is the law of symmetry, the rule of equilibrium. And if one side of this directionality were to lose its other side, then the equilibrium would be destroyed and the universe would be upended. Every phenomenon has a phenomenon opposite and equal to itself. Every thesis, an antithesis. That which is infinite upwards is infinite downwards, that which is finite upwards is of course finite downwards. And until this point in time, the year 1932, this law has not been violated. We have observed no upper limit to rising temperature, but we do know the lower limit, which is absolute zero—273°. But we have yet to reach that point. No matter how close we might have approached it, we have yet to reach it. And we do not know what happens with nature, when it does achieve this limit. This constitutes a very interesting problem: in order that a lower limit be reached, one needs to presuppose the existence of an upper limit. In the opposite case, we would be forced to make the following conclusions: either the upper limit after all exists somewhere, but is still unknown to us, or the temperature of 273° is not the lower limit or, having reached the lower limit, nature is so much transformed that it, for all intents and purposes, ceases to exist, or that the theorem of the ends of infinity is false. In the last case, the situation is such: 'something had no beginning and will have no end' may not be considered to be 'something had no beginning and therefore will have no end' and that the infinity of two directions would seem to have ceased being nothing and has now become something. We would have caught infinity by the tail."

I wrote this with some interruptions, then reread it with great interest, and continued reasoning in the following manner:

"Here is the set of numbers. We do not know what these are, but we see that, due to certain of their qualities, they can be distributed in a strict, clearly defined order. And some of us even think that numbers are but an expression of this order, and that outside such an order, the existence of numbers is senseless. But this order is such that in its beginning it presupposes a unit. And this unit is followed by another, and so on, without end. The numbers express this order: 1, 2, 3, etc. And so, before us is a model of a unidirectional infinity. This is an infinity without equilibrium. In one of its directions it has an end, in the other direction it doesn't. Something had a beginning somewhere and did not end anywhere, and it pierced us with its beginning, starting at the number one. Several numbers from among the first ten became part of the circle of our consciousness and united us with eternity. But our minds were incapable of tolerating this and we balanced the infinite sequence of numbers with another infinite sequence of numbers, created along the principle of the first, but distributed from the beginning of the first in the opposite direction. The point of conjunction of these two sequences, the first natural and incomprehensible, the second patently invented, but explaining the first, this point of their conjunction we called zero. And so the set of numbers has no point of beginning and no ending. It became nothing. This would all seem to be true, but everything here is disrupted by the zero. It stands somewhere in the middle of the infinite set and qualitatively differs from it. That which we had called nothing contains in itself something else which, by comparison with this nothing, is a new nothing. Two nothings? Two nothings and each in contradiction with the other? And one of the nothings is something. Then, this nothing, which doesn't begin anywhere and has no place where it ends, is something, containing a nothing in itself."

I read what I had written and thought for a long time. Then I did not think for several days. And then I became immersed in thought again. I was fascinated with numbers and I thought the following:

"We imagine numbers to ourselves as certain properties of the relationships of certain properties of things. And, in such a fashion, numbers were created by things."

And this made me realize that this was idiotic, my reasoning was idiotic. I swung open the window and began to stare out into the yard. Promenading in the yard, I saw cocks and hens.

Kursk, August 2, 1932

Himmelkumov was staring at a young lady . . .

Himmelkumov was staring at a young lady in the window opposite his. But the young lady in the window opposite did not look at Himmelkumov even once. "She's just being bashful," Himmelkumov thought to himself.

Himmelkumov painted his face with green mascara and came to the window. "Let them all think: what a strange man," Himmelkumov was saying to himself.

There was no more tobacco and Himmelkumov had nothing to smoke. He sucked on the empty pipe, but this only intensified the torment. So two hours passed. And then the miraculous tobacco appeared.

Himmelkumov bugged out his eyes at the young lady and was willing her to turn her head. However, this did not help. Then Himmelkumov tried to will the young lady not to look at him. This didn't help either.

Himmelkumov was searching for an internal idea he could immerse himself in for the span of his entire lifetime. It is pleasant to be concentrated all in one point like a madman. Everywhere and in everything such a person sees his own object. Everything is his great pleasure. Everything bears a direct relationship to his beloved object.

Suddenly, Himmelkumov was overcome with a wave of insatiable gluttony. But toward what object this sense of greed was directed was unclear. Himmelkumov repeated to himself the rules of hyphenation and for a long time pondered the letters "s," "t," "v," which are invisible. "Of late, I am particularly avaricious," Himmelkumov was saying to himself. A flea was biting him; he was scratching himself and splitting in his head the word "essence," so as to carry it over from one line to another.

[*1933*]

From the Notebooks (1933, 1935)

September 21 [1933]

Interesting thing: German, Frenchman, American, Japanese, Hindu, Jew, even Samoyed—all these are definite nouns, like the old-style *rossiyanin*. For the new era, there is no participial noun for a "Rus-Man." There is the word "*russkii*," a participial derived from an adjective, and it even sounds like an adjective. The Rus-Man has yet to find his determination! Even less defined, however, is the "Soviet Man."* How sensitive words are!

On Laughter

1. Advice to artist-humorists

   I have noticed that it is very important to identify what it is that produces laughter. If you want to make your audience laugh, walk out on the stage and stand silent until someone begins to laugh. Then wait a little longer, until another starts laughing, but make sure that everyone hears this one. Only this laughter will be genuine, and the clappers are useless in this instance. Once all this has taken place, know that a pretext for laughter has been established. After this, you may proceed with your comedic routine, resting easy that your success is assured.

2. There are several sorts of laughter. There is your average sort of laughter, when the entire room is laughing, but not all out. And there is the strong sort of laughter, when only one part of the room is laughing, but those who are, are splitting at the

---

* This presciently anticipates the coining of the term "Homo Sovieticus."

seams and the other part remains silent; the humor in this entirely escapes them. The first sort of laughter is what the entertainment committee requires of the stage actor, but the second is better. The cattle should not be permitted to low.

September 25 [1933]

On Being Prolific

One should never confuse the difference between being productive and prolific. The first is not always good; the second is good always.

My creations are my dear sons and daughters. It is better to sire three strong sons than forty middling.

Do not mistake prolific for productive. Prolific is the capacity to leave a strong and enduring legacy, and productive is merely the capacity to leave a numerous legacy that may survive a long time, but that might also quickly die out.

A man possessing proliferative force is also usually simultaneously productive.

October 20, 1933

On Geniuses

If we exclude the ancients, about whom I am unable to conjecture, then genuine geniuses are only five in number, and two of them are Russian. Here are the five poet-geniuses:

Dante, Shakespeare, Goethe, Pushkin, and Gogol.

———

It is better to pronounce a middling thing good than to slander the good, and therefore I proclaim that Shostakovich must be a genius. Having heard the first two acts of his opera *Lady Macbeth*, I am inclined to believe that Shostakovich is no genius.

Oct. 20 [1933]

————

Jean-Baptiste Poquelin Molière
I closely inspected one of the three extant signatures of Molière, from the year 1668.

It is a gorgeous, precise signature, not one of the letters written without due attention.

The signature in its entirety looks like this:

————

I have studied women for a long time now and can definitively say that I know them with flying colors. First and foremost, a woman likes to be attended to. Let's say she is standing right in front of you or is about to, and you make it seem as though you're hearing and seeing nothing, and act like there's no one else in the room; this inflames female curiosity. And a curious woman is capable of practically anything.

The next time I will intentionally stick my hand deep in my pocket with a quizzical appearance, and the woman will plant her eyes on me, like, what's going on here? And I will slowly draw out of my pocket some sort of spark plug. Well and good; the trap has been sprung, and the fish is in my net!

————

July 1935

One of the principal sources of divergence of human paths is the matter of preference for either skinny or plump women.

I propose we reserve alleys in public gardens for quiet strolling, with two-seat benches distributed two meters away from each other; furthermore, thick bushes should be planted between the benches so that those sitting at one bench are not able to see what is happening at another. On these quiet pathways, the following rules must be enforced:

1. Entrance is forbidden to children, both alone and accompanied by a parent.
2. All noise and loud conversation are strictly prohibited.
3. Only one woman may take a seat next to a man, and only one man next to a woman.
4. If the person seated on a bench is resting their hand or some sort of other object on the free seat, you may not join them.

Alleys should also be reserved for walking in solitude, with metal armchairs for single people. Between the armchairs, bushes. Entry is forbidden to children; noise and loud conversation are prohibited.

———

As a rule, pretty women do not stroll around in gardens.

Selected Prose from the Middle Years

✦ 1933–1938 ✦

Two Letters to Klavdia Vasilyevna [Pugacheva]

1

October 5, 1933

Dear Klavdia Vasilyevna,

more than anything in the world, I wish to see you. You have absolutely beguiled me. I am very grateful to you for your letter. I think of you all the time. And it seems to me again that you have moved to Moscow for nothing. I love the theater very much, but, regrettably, there's no such thing as theater today. The time of theater, of grand epic poems, of beautiful architecture came to an end one hundred years ago. Do not deceive yourself into thinking that Khlebnikov wrote any major poems. And Meyerhold—he, at least, stands for theater.

Khlebnikov is the best poet of the second half of the XIXth, first quarter of the XXth c., yet his long poems are nothing more than extended verses; and Meyerhold, he hasn't done much of anything.

I firmly believe that the time of great poems, architecture, and theater will return one day. But it's not that time yet. Until new paradigms are established in these three arts, the tested, true methods remain the best. If I were you, I would either attempt to create a new theater, if you felt in yourself greatness sufficient for such a task, or stick to the theater of the most archaic kind.

By the way, the Children's Theater is in much better shape than the one for grown-ups. Even if not plowing up fertile ground for a New Age, at least it is not a condition specific to the juvenile audience—

though it is muddled through with "theatrical science," "Constructivism," and "Leftism" (don't forget that I myself have been labeled among the "leftmost of poets")—it is still the purest of all the other theaters.

Dear Klavdia Vasilyevna, how regrettable it is that you've left our fair city, all the more a pity because I've become attached to you with all my soul. I wish you, darling Klavdia Vasilyevna, success in all your endeavors.

Daniil Kharms

2

Monday
October 16, 1933
Petersburg

Talent grows, destroying, building.
The sign of stagnation is well-being.

Dear Klavdia Vasilyevna,

You are a remarkable and genuine person!

As much as it grieves me not to be able to see you, I won't be inviting you to the Children's Theater or to come to my city. How heartwarming it is to know that there still exists one human being animated by dreams! I don't know what word one can use to express that force which so delights me in you. I usually call it simply p u r i t y.

I have been thinking about how wonderful it is, that which is primal! How wonderful unmediated reality is! How wonderful sun and grass and stone and water and birds and the beetle and the fly and a man. But a shot glass and knife or key and comb are just as beautiful. If I were to go blind and lose my hearing and all my senses, then how could I possibly lose all this beauty? Everything has vanished and there is nothing left for me anymore. But here, I've been given back my sense of touch, and almost immediately the whole world has re-appeared. I acquired hearing, and the world became significantly better yet. I got back all my other senses and the world was better still. The world began to exist, as soon as I allowed it inside myself. Granted it may still be in disarray, but at least it is! However, I then began to put the world in order. And now Art has made its appearance with us. Only then did I understand the distinction between the sun and the comb, but at the same time, I realized that these two are one and the same.

Now my task is to create the proper order. I am preoccupied with this and it is everything I think about. I talk about it, attempt to relate, describe, sketch it, dance it, construct it. I am the creator of the world, and this is the most important thing about me. How could I possibly not think about it all the time! Everything I do, I infuse with the thought that I am the world's creator. And I'm not simply making a boot but, first and foremost, I create a new thing. It's not sufficient for me to turn out a boot that is comfortable, durable, and beautiful. It is important that this boot exhibit the same order which is in the whole world: so that the world's order not be sullied, soiled by contact with nail and skin, so that, despite the boot's form, it would retain its own form, remain as it has been, that it remain p u r e.

This is that same purity which permeates all art. When I write poems, what seems most important to me is not the idea, not the content or form, nor that nebulous concept we call "quality," but something even hazier and more incomprehensible to the rational mind, but which is clear to me and, I hope, to you as well, dearest Klavdia Vasilyevna, this p u r i t y of o r d e r.

This purity is one and the same as the one in the sun, and in the grass, in a person, and in poems. Genuine art stands in the order of the set of primary reality, it creates the world and it is its first reflection. It is absolutely real.

But, dear Lord, what trifles genuine art consists of. *The Divine Comedy* is a great work but Pushkin's "The moon is rising through the misty waters" is no less wonderful. For both the one and the other contain that purity, and consequently, the same proximity to reality, i.e., towards independent existence. These are no longer mere words and thoughts printed on paper, it is a thing just as real as the crystal inkwell which stands before me on my writing desk. It seems to me these verses, that have become a thing, may be lifted off the paper and flung at the window, and the glass will shatter. This is what words are capable of!

But on the other hand, how pitiable and helpless these same words may be! I never read the newspapers. This is a fictitious and not a created world. It is nothing but pathetic, worndown type, offset on poor quality, splintery paper.

Does man require anything in life besides art? I think not: he needs nothing else, it encompasses everything that is real.

I think purity may be found in all things, even in how a man eats his soup. I think you did the right thing, coming to Moscow. You're able to take walks in the streets and act in a starving theater. There's more purity in that than living here, in this comfortable room, acting in a children's theater.

I am always suspicious of all good fortune. Today, Zabolotsky came to visit me. He's been taking a keen interest in architecture for a long time now and has written a long poem,* in which he's expressed many wonderful thoughts about architecture and human life. I know that many people will be amazed by it. But I also know it is a bad poem. Only in several places, almost accidentally, is it good. These are two separate categories.

The first category is comprehensible and simple. Here, everything is so clear that one knows exactly what one is supposed to do. It's understood: what one must pursue and how this may be accomplished. Here, the way is apparent. This is fertile ground for discussion; and one day, a literary critic will write an entire tome on the

---

* We may presume that this reference is to Nikolay Zabolotsky's lost poem "Clouds" (1933). Zabolotsky, Kharms's fellow OBERIU member, was the most widely recognized of the group, universally acknowledged as a major poet.

subject, and a commentator six volumes, explaining and interpreting it. Here, everything is as it should be.

Of the second category [the ineffable], no one will utter a word, even though it is precisely what makes architecture and all our thoughts about human life beautiful. It's incomprehensible, insensible, and at the same time wonderful, this second category! But it can't be achieved, it is foolish to even seek it, there are no paths leading to it. It is precisely this second category which forces a man to suddenly drop everything and take up mathematics, and then, after having abandoned math, suddenly take up Arab music, and then get married, and then, having sliced up his wife and son, lie in the field on his stomach examining a flower.

Yes, this is the most unfortunate of categories, which makes a man a genius.

(By the way, I'm no longer talking here about Zabolotsky, who's yet to slaughter his wife, or take up mathematics.)

Dear Klavdia Vasilyevna, I am not at all making fun of your visits to the zoo. There was a time when I too visited our local zoological garden daily. I'd made there the acquaintance of a particular wolf and a pelican. If you allow me, I will one day tell you in detail how splendidly we'd passed the time together.

If you'd like, I will describe for you how I once lived an entire summer at the Lakhtinsky zoological station, in the castle of Count Stenbock-Fermora, living on a diet of live worms and Nestlé's milk powder, in the company of a nearly mad zoologist, spiders, ants, and snakes.

I'm genuinely delighted that you take your walks like so, in the Zoological Garden. Especially if you take walks there not just for the sake of walking, but also to observe the animals—I will fall in love with you even more tenderly.

Daniil Kharms

Letter to Anonymous, in Kursk

Dear Doctor,

It made me so very very happy to receive your letter. Those few conversations, quite fragmentary and therefore unreliable, which we had, you and me, remain very much in my memory, and this reminiscence is the only consolation of my time in Kursk. What can I say, dear Doctor, but you must absolutely get out of that cabbage patch. You recall how, in the Bible, God spares an entire city for the sake of a single righteous man. So, thanks to you, I too can't enjoy the guilty pleasure of bad-mouthing Kursk. To this day I refer to you as the "Good Doctor," but there is no longer anything medical about this: it is more in line with "Doctor Faust." There is so much left in you that is German, not Gaul (*hosen*, *pfeffer*, *bratwurst*, etc.), but genuine German *Geist*, so like an organ. The Russian spirit sings as a church choir, or like some nasal two-bit deacon—the Russian spirit. This is always either divine, or entirely laughable. But the German *Geist* is an organ. You are able to say of nature: "I love nature. See that cedar, it is very beautiful. One might find a knight standing under such a tree, and over there, on that mountain, you may see a monk taking his stroll." Such sensations are entirely foreign to me. For me, either a table or a scale, rafters or a meadow, grove or a grasshopper, or butterfly—they are all one unified thing.

[*1933?*]

Then everyone began to speak in their own private language . . .

Then everyone began to speak in their own private language.

Khvilischevsky approached a tree and scratched into its bark. An ant emerged out of the bark and fell to the ground. Khvilischevsky bent down, but the ant was no longer to be seen.

At the same time, Fakirov was pacing back and forth. Fakirov's face bore a strict, even menacing expression. Fakirov was trying to walk in a straight line, and when he reached the house, he immediately made a sharp turnaround.

Khvilischevsky was still standing by the tree and examining the bark through his pince-nez with his nearsighted eyes. Khvilischevsky's neck was wrinkled and thin.

Then everyone began speaking about numbers.

Khvilischevsky averred that such a number is familiar to everyone, that if it were written in the Chinese manner, from top to bottom, it would resemble a baker.

Nonsense—said Fakirov—why a baker?

You try it yourself and you will be convinced—said Khvilischevsky, swallowing a drop of his spit, which caused his collar to jump up and his tie to slide over to one side.

Alright then, what number is it? Fakirov asked, reaching for a pencil.

Please understand, I keep this number a secret—said Khvilischevsky.

Who knows how all this would have ended, but just then Voluman [Uemov] entered, bringing with him much news.

Fakirov sat in his sky-blue velvet jacket smoking a pipe.

Numbers are such an important part of nature! Height and action, everything is a number.

And the word is a force.

Number and word are our mother!

October 5 [1933–34]

A little old man was scratching himself . . .

A little old man was scratching himself with both hands. Where he could not reach with both hands, the old man scratched with one hand only, but quickly-quickly and then, the whole time, while rapidly blinking his eyes.

———

Steam, or what we call smoke, was pouring out of the locomotive's blast pipe. And a festively feathered bird, flying through this smoke, came out of it stringy and disheveled.

———

Khvilischevsky was eating raw cranberries and trying very hard not to wince. He was expecting any second someone to say: "What strength of character!" But no one said a thing.

———

You could hear the dog sniffing around outside the door. Khvilischevsky was clutching a toothbrush in his balled-up fist and bugging his eyes out so as to hear better. "If the dog comes in," Khvilischevsky was thinking to himself, "I will thrash it right on the temple, with this bone handle!"

———

. . . Some sort of bubbles were issuing out of the box. Khvilischevsky departed from the room on tiptoes, closing the door behind him silently. "To heck with it!" Khvilischevsky said to himself. "It's no concern of mine, what's inside the box. Come on, really! To hell with it!"

Khvilischevsky meant to cry out: "Don't enter!" But his tongue had somehow deceived him and what came out was: "Done empty." Khvilischevsky squinted with his right eye and, with a look of mighty distinction, strode out of the reception hall. But still, he had a niggling suspicion that he had heard Tsuckerman snicker.

[*1933–34*]

Andrey Semeonovich spat into a cup . . .

Andrey Semeonovich spat into a cup full of water. The water immediately turned black. Andrey Semeonovich squinted his eyes and looked at the cup up close. The water was very black. Andrey Semeonovich's heart began to pound.

At that moment, Andrey Semeonovich's dog woke up. Andrey Semeonovich approached the window and became submerged in thought.

All of a sudden something large and dark hurtled past Andrey Semeonovich's face and flew out the window. It was Andrey Semeonovich's dog that flew past and raced like a crow to the roof of the building on the opposite side of the street. Andrey Semeonovich's dog squatted down and began to howl.

Comrade Popugaev* ran into the room.

What is going on with you? Are you ill? Comrade Popugaev asked.

Andrey Semeonovich remained silent and rubbed his face with his hands.

Comrade Popugaev glanced into the cup standing on the table.

What is it you have poured in here? he asked Andrey Semeonovich.

I don't know, said Andrey Semeonovich.

And in a jiffy, Popugaev vanished. The dog flew back in through the window, lay down in its usual place, and fell asleep.

Andrey Semeonovich walked over to the table and drank from the cup of the blackened water.

And Andrey Semeonovich's soul grew lighter.

August 21 [*1934*]

---

* *Popugaev*: literally, "Parrotman."

I was born among the cattails . . .

I was born among the cattails. Like a mouse. My mother gave birth to me and placed me in the water. And I swam off.

Some kind of fish with four whiskers on its nose circled around me. I started to cry. And the fish started to cry also.

All of a sudden we saw, swimming on the surface, a porridge. We ate the porridge and started to laugh.

We were very happy and we swam along with the current and met a lobster. This was an ancient, giant lobster and he was holding in his claws an ax.

Swimming behind the lobster was a naked frog.

Why are you always naked? the lobster asked her. How come you aren't ashamed?

There is nothing shameful in this, the frog said. Why should we be ashamed of our beautiful bodies, given to us by nature, when we aren't ashamed of our despicable deeds, that we ourselves create?

You speak the truth, said the lobster. And I don't know how to give you an answer to this. I propose that we ask a human being, because a human being is smarter than we are. Because we are wise only in fables, which human beings compose about us, so that it again appears here that the human being is wise and not we. So that's when the lobster saw me and said:

And we don't even have to swim anywhere because here's one—a human.

The lobster swam up alongside me and asked:

Should one be ashamed of one's own naked body? You are a human so tell us.

I am a human being and I will answer your question: we should not be ashamed of our naked bodies.

[*1934?*]

Olga Forsh approached Alexei Tolstoy . . .

Olga Forsh approached Alexei Tolstoy* and did something.

Alexei Tolstoy did something too.

Then Konstantin Fedin and Valentin Stenich ran out into the yard and began searching for an appropriate stone. They didn't find a stone, but they did find a shovel. With this shovel, Konstantin Fedin smacked Olga Forsh across her mug.

Then Alexei Tolstoy stripped off all his clothes and completely naked walked out onto the Fontanka and began to neigh like a horse. Everybody was saying: "There neighing is a major contemporary writer." And no one even lay a hand on Alexei Tolstoy.

[*1934*]

---

* Alexei Tolstoy, or "Comrade Count," beloved writer of children's fairy tales, sci-fi, and historical romances, famously returned from exile to assume a leading role in the Writers' Union. Olga Forsh, Konstantin Fedin, and Valentin Stenich, immensely popular writers in their own right, were all important members of the Writers' Union. This anecdote refers to Osip Mandelstam's famous "slap in the face of public taste." Nadezhda Mandelstam's *Hope Against Hope* begins, "After slapping Alexei Tolstoy in the face, M. immediately returned to Moscow."

I can't imagine why, but everyone thinks I'm a genius . . .

I can't imagine why, but everyone thinks I'm a genius; but if you ask me, I'm no genius. Just yesterday I was telling them: Please hear me! What sort of a genius am I? And they tell me: What a genius! And I tell them: Well, what kind? But they don't tell me what kind, they only repeat, genius this, genius that. But if you ask me, I'm no genius at all.

Wherever I go, immediately they all start whispering and pointing their fingers at me. What's going on here?! I say. But they don't let me utter a word, and any minute now they will lift me up in the air and carry me off on their shoulders.

[1934–36]

The Personal Inner Turmoil
of a Certain Musician

They called me a pervert.

Ain't that the truth?

No, it's not. I'm not about to start exonerating myself here by offering evidence in my defense.

* * *

I heard how my wife was speaking into the telephone receiver with a certain Mikhusya; what am I, a fool?

I was sitting at the time under the bed so I wouldn't be seen.

Oh, what I was feeling in that moment!

I wanted to jump out and scream: "No, I'm no fool!"

I can just imagine what would've happened.

* * *

I was again sitting under the bed and was invisible.

But I could see what this Mikhusya was doing to my wife.

* * *

Today, my wife was yet again receiving this Mikhusya.

I'm beginning to think that, in my wife's eyes, I'm beginning to play second fiddle.

I myself was sitting under the bed and invisible.

Mikhusya was even rummaging around in the drawers of my writing desk.

* * *

I sat again under the bed and was invisible.

The wife and Mikhusya were talking about me in the most unflattering terms.

I couldn't take it any longer and yelled out to them that they were lying through their teeth.

* * *

It's already the fifth day since I was beaten up, but my bones are still hurting.

[1935–36]

A Knight in Shining Armor

Alexei Alexeevich Alexeev was a genuine knight in shining armor. For example, one time, seeing from a passing tram how one lady who, having tripped over a flowerpot, dropped a glass lampshade for a table lamp out of her shopping bag so that it immediately shattered, Alexei Alexeevich, wishing to come to the lady's aid, decided to sacrifice himself and, jumping off the tram going at full speed, fell and split his face against a rock. Another time, seeing how one lady, climbing over a fence, had got her skirt snagged on a nail and was stuck in such a position that, sitting on top of the fence, she could move neither back nor forward, Alexei Alexeevich became so agitated that, as a result of his emotional tension, he forced the front two teeth out of his mouth with his tongue. Simply put, Alexei Alexeevich was a most genuine knight in shining armor, and not only in his relations with the ladies. With unheard of levity, Alexei Alexeevich was willing to sacrifice himself for the Faith, Tsar, and Fatherland, something he proved in 1914, and the beginning of the German War, by throwing himself, with the yell of "For the Motherland!" down into the street out of a third-story window. By some miracle, Alexei Alexeevich survived, having gotten off with only some minor bruises, and soon, being such a remarkably zealous patriot extraordinaire, he was called up to the front.

At the front, Alexei Alexeevich distinguished himself by his elevated sentiments and, each time that he pronounced the words "banner," "fanfare," and even simply "epaulets," a tear of endearment came trickling down his face.

In the year 1916, Alexei Alexeevich was wounded in the loins and evacuated from the front.

As a Category I disabled war veteran, Alexei Alexeevich did not have to work and, making use of his free time, formulated his patriotic sentiments on paper.

One time, engaged in a conversation with Konstantin Lebedev, Alexei Alexeevich quoted his favorite phrase: "I suffered for my native land by sacrificing my loins, but live with the strength of the convictions of my posterior subconscious."

"You're an idiot!" Konstantin Lebedev said to him. "Only a LIBERAL may serve his country to the fullest measure."

For some reason, these words made a deep impression on Alexei Alexeevich's soul, and by the year 1917 we already found him calling himself "a liberal who sacrificed his loins for his fatherland."

Alexei Alexeevich welcomed the revolution with fervor, even though he was deprived of his pension. For a period of time, Konstantin Lebedev provisioned him with cane sugar, chocolate, canned pig fat, and cracked wheat. But when Konstantin Lebedev disappeared suddenly and without a trace, Alexei Alexeevich was obliged to go out in the street and beg for handouts. At first, Alexei Alexeevich would stretch out his hand and say: "Please give, for Christ's sake, to one who sacrificed his loins for his native land." But this did not meet with approbation. And so Alexei Alexeevich substituted for the word "country" the word "revolution." But this also did not prove a success. Then Alexei Alexeevich composed a revolutionary song and, seeing a person, who in the opinion of Alexei Alexeevich was able to give alms, coming down the street, would make a step forward and, with an expression of pride and dignity on his face, flinging his head backward begin to sing:

> To the barricades
> We all will stream
> And for our freedom
> We will all be crippled and killed!

And with great panache, in the Polish style, clicking his heels, Alexei Alexeevich would hold out his hat and say: "Please give alms, for Christ's sake." This helped, and Alexei Alexeevich rarely had to go without food again.

Everything went well, but in 1922, Alexei Alexeevich became acquainted with a person named Ivan Ivanovich Puzyrev [Bubble-man], who sold sunflower oil at the Straw Market. Puzyrev invited Alexei Alexeevich to a café and treated him to some real coffee and, while stuffing himself with pastries, spelled out some sort of complicated scheme, from which Alexei Alexeevich understood only what he was supposed to do, for which part he would receive from Puzyrev provisions of food. Alexei Alexeevich agreed and Puzyrev immediately, as a form of recompense, passed to him under the table two packets of tea and a pack of Radja cigarettes.

From this day forth, every morning Alexei Alexeevich came to see Puzyrev at the market and, receiving from him some sort of papers with scribbled signatures and innumerable official stamps, took a sled, if this was happening in winter, or, if it was happening in summer, a hand cart and set off, according to Puzyrev's instructions, on the rounds of various offices where, having displayed his papers, he received some sort of boxes which he loaded on his sled or hand cart and, in the evening, would cart them off to Puzyrev at the latter's apartment. However, one time, as Alexei Alexeevich was pulling his sled up to Puzyrev's house, two men, one of them wearing a military overcoat, approached and asked him: "Is your last name Alexeev?" Later, Alexei Alexeevich was deposited in an automobile and hauled off to jail.

Under questioning, Alexei Alexeevich understood not a thing and only repeated that he had sacrificed his loins for his country and for the revolution. Still, despite this, he was sentenced to ten years exile to the northernmost regions of his fatherland. Having returned back to Leningrad in 1928, Alexei Alexeevich resumed his former occupation and, standing on the corner of Volodarsky Prospect, threw his head back and, with an expression of pride, stomped his heels and began to sing:

To the barricades
We all will stream
And for our freedom
We will all be crippled and killed!

But without having completed his song even a second time, he was carted off in an unmarked car somewhere in the direction of the Admiralty. That was the last time anyone saw him.

And so ends this brief account of the life of that most distinguished knight and patriot, Alexei Alexeevich Alexeev.

[*1934–36*]

The window, shuttered with a curtain . . .

The window, shuttered with a curtain, was growing lighter and lighter, because the day had begun. The floors had begun to creak, doors to sing, the chairs were being shuffled in their apartments. Ruzhetskii, climbing out of his bed, fell on the floor and cracked his face open. He was in a hurry to get to work and therefore went out in the street having only covered his face with his hands. His hands were making it difficult for Ruzhetskii to see the way, and for this reason he twice collided with an advertising arcade and shoved some old man who was wearing a felt hat with long furry earflaps, which brought the geezer into such a state of rage that a street sweeper, who had just happened to be nearby and was attempting to catch a tomcat with a shovel, had to calm the old man down: "Aren't you ashamed, grandpa, to be, at your age, behaving like a teenage hooligan."

[*1935*]

An Unexpected Binge

One time, Antonina Alexeevna struck her husband with an official seal and smeared his forehead with ink from a stamping pad.

This insulted Pyotr Leonidovich, Antonina Alexeevna's husband, terribly, and he locked himself in the bathroom and would not allow anyone to enter.

However, the inhabitants of the communal apartment, having a strong urge to go there where Pyotr Leonidovich was sitting, decided to force the locked door open.

Seeing that his case was lost, Pyotr Leonidovich exited the bathroom and, striding to his room, lay down there, in his bed.

But Antonina Alexeevna decided to pursue her husband to the end. She shredded some paper into tiny pieces and scattered them over Pyotr Leonidovich lying there in his bed.

Pyotr Leonidovich burst into the hallway enraged and proceeded to tear into the wallpaper.

At the sight of this, all the neighbors ran into the hallway and set upon him, tearing his vest to pieces. Pyotr Leonidovich ran off to the management office.

At the same time, Antonina Alexeevna stripped herself bare and hid in a trunk.

In ten minutes, Pyotr Leonidovich returned, with the building superintendent in tow.

Not finding his wife in the room, the building super and Pyotr Leonidovich decided to use the opportunity presented to them by the empty apartment to drink a little vodka. Pyotr Leonidovich took it upon himself to run out to the corner store for this beverage.

When Pyotr Leonidovich had left, Antonina Alexeevna popped out from the trunk and appeared before the building super in all her splendor.

The superintendent, all shook up, jumped up from his chair and raced to the window, but catching an eyeful of the powerful figure of the twenty-six-year-young woman, suddenly worked himself up into a frenzy.

That's when Pyotr Leonidovich returned with a bottle of vodka.

Getting an inkling of what was going on in his room, Pyotr Leonidovich knitted his eyebrows.

But his spouse, Antonina Alexeevna, flashed him with the official seal and Pyotr Leonidovich calmed down.

Antonina Alexeevna expressed her desire to take part in the binge, but as a matter of course, in the nude and while sitting on the table to boot, on which it was also proposed to make a spread of the zakuski and the vodka.

The men sat on chairs, and Antonina Alexeevna sat on the table, and the drunken binge began.

One could hardly call this hygienic, when a naked young woman is sitting on the same table that people are eating from. On top of it, Antonina Alexeevna was a rather plump in build woman and not particularly scrupulous in her personal habits, so that it was all . . . God only knows.

Soon, however, all of them were sloshed and asleep, the men on the floor and Antonina Alexeevna on the table.

And so, once again, an orderly silence descended upon the communal apartment.

Jan. 22, 1935

A Terrifying Death

Once upon a time, a man, feeling hungry, sat at the table and ate cutlets.

Beside him sat his wife, rambling on about the cutlets not containing enough pork.

Nevertheless, he ate, and ate, and ate, and ate, and ate, until he sensed somewhere in the pit of his stomach a morbid heaviness.

In that moment, having moved aside the food, he began to tremble and cry.

The gold watch in his pocket ceased to tick.

His hair suddenly lightened a shade, and his vision brightened.

His ears tumbled to the floor, as in autumn the yellow leaves drop from the poplars, and he fell down dead.

[April 1935]

Sweet Little Lida

Sweet Little Lida was squatting and digging in the sand with a wooden cup.

On the bench beside her sat a broad-shouldered girl with puffy lips and thick calves. This was Anyuta, Little Lida's nanny. Usually, a military man would be sidling up to her, holding her hands, and so they sat while Little Lida played in the sand. But this time, for some reason, the soldier did not come and Anyuta was sitting on the bench, one leg placed over the other, looking at the men passing by with malice in her eye.

Little Lida tossed the sand in the air. The sand scattered in the air and hit the nanny in the eye.

Lida! Don't dare throw the sand again! Anyuta yelled.

Little Lida intentionally tossed another fistful of the sand upward.

Anyuta jumped up from the bench, grabbed Little Lida by the hand, and dragged her to the exit. Little Lida walked behind Anyuta in silence.

A little dog wearing a collar made of little bells trotted by. Little Lida wanted to stop to look at the dog, but Anyuta jerked Little Lida by the hand and led her onward.

There's no need to stop for every dog, the nanny was saying, dragging Little Lida toward the exit.

Little Lida was mad, but realizing that Anyuta was stronger, walked on in submission, only trying to shuffle up with her right foot as much dust from the path as possible.

At the very exit, they were approached by the soldier who usually sidled up to Anyuta and took her hands in his. Seeing the soldier, Anyuta let Little Lida's little hand drop from hers and headed toward the soldier, adjusting her skirt as she walked.

Little Lida bolted out of the playground and ran along the sidewalk. An old woman with a basket which contained red hard candy and glazed biscuits, seeing Little Lida, clapped her hands and yelled:

Where! Where are you going? What's the rush?

Lidochka crossed a little bridge, stumbled over some sort of wooden stake, bumped into someone's leg, turned the corner of some house, and suddenly saw in front of her an entirely unfamiliar street.

Lidochka wanted to turn back, but a dump truck backed out of the gates of a house, parked across the sidewalk, and blocked her way.

Little Lida shuffled her feet in place, blinked her eyes, and suddenly began to cry very loudly.

Little girl! Little girl! Why are you crying? Don't cry, missus! Come with me and I'll give you some chocolates.

Little Lida raised her eyes and saw before her a little old man with gold-rimmed glasses, a white newsboy's cap, a checkered jacket covered with fat stains, and knicker-length pants from under which stuck out dirty knee-high silk socks, bright green in color.

Come with me, little missus, to my house and we will take care of you! the old man was saying, wiggling his little, gray barbed mustaches and little goatee beard reminiscent of a swallow's tail.

The little old man held his arm out toward her and took Little Lida around the shoulders.

Little girl! Little girl! Come with me, quicker. We'll find our papa and mama and bring you home, the old man was saying, gently shoving Lidochka toward his house. The old man's hands were shaking. The old man kept grabbing Little Lida, first by the head, then around the shoulders, then directly by her chin. The old man smelled of aftershave and of the tub in which they wash dirty laundry. He was taking quick little steps and, the whole time pushing Little Lida ahead, arrived with her in tow in the foyer of an apartment building.

I don't want to go in there! Little Lida screamed.

From the street, a woman with a briefcase under her arm glanced inside the entryway.

The little old man smiled in the lady's direction and, tightening his fingers around Little Lida's neck, said:

My dumpling! Dumpling! No more temper tantrums. You've gotten your little feet wet, so let's quickly go upstairs and eat some porridge. Don't you see, daddy loves you very much!

And so, despite Lidochka's resistance he proceeded to pull her up the staircase.

Little Lida began to scream but the little old man clapped her mouth shut with the palm of his hand. Little Lida heard how the little old man fumbled and huffed by the door, struggling to open it without letting Little Lida out of his hands. Then Little Lida was raised up in the air, carried several steps, and deposited on something prickly and rough. Little Lida opened her eyes and saw herself seated on an old velour sofa, in a long narrow room with dirty bare walls and a gray, crackling ceiling. Besides the sofa, the room contained an oversized bow-legged armchair with a wooden seat and two folding card tables. One of the tables was covered with a pile of dirty old rags and the other with chipped, unwashed dishes that contained the remnants of food. There was nothing else in the room, if one were not to count the huge mirror hanging on the wall, cracked its entire length and glued with a stripe of yellow paper, and a stinking pail between the window and the couch, and the used matches and stubbed-out cigarette butts and empty cans scattered around everywhere on the floor. In the room, even though it was daytime, the electric light was on and a bare, low-wattage bulb hung from the ceiling. The window was covered with a thick woolen blanket.

The little old man was standing above the sofa and, like a rabbit with its lips, mustache, and mouth slowly twitching, looked at Little Lida.

Little Lida sat down on the couch and was about to start crying but the little old man again clamped his hand down over her mouth and hissed:

If you cry, little miss, I will make you hurt so bad, I will tear your little head off. You will die and your mama will never see you again.

Little Lida began to cry. The little old man crushed down on her mouth even harder. Little Lida began to struggle, but the little old man pushed her down on the sofa and stuck his dirty finger into her mouth. Lidochka let out a piercing scream. But the little old man stuck his finger straight down her throat and she gagged and began to cough.

Silence! said the little old man and suddenly added in a terrifying voice: If you scream, I will begin to tear you into pieces!

The voice was so horrible that Little Lida grew quiet.

The little old man sat down on the sofa next to Little Lida.

So here we are—the little old man said, passing his stinking fingers with their long brown nails over Little Lida's face. And you, little missus, have calmed down. You, little missus, are afraid of me for no reason. I am so very, very kind. And my name is Uncle Mika. Uncle Mika loves little missuses like yourself. Uncle Mika plays different games with little missuses like yourself, and gives little missuses delicious chocolate bonbons. Uncle Mika is oh so very kind. And now kind Uncle Mika will undress the little missus and put her all naked on a silk pillow.

With these words, Uncle Mika began to undress Lidochka. Little Lida was so scared that she remained silent and didn't resist. Uncle Mika took off her little dress, and her little shirt, and her little pants, and Little Lida was left completely naked, in only her little shoes and little socks.

The little old man threw himself on Little Lida and it seemed to Lidochka that he would now bite her on her stomach. Little Lida screamed. Immediately, Uncle Mika stuck his finger in her mouth.

Be quiet! screamed Uncle Mika, and in a gentle voice added: And if the little missus doesn't keep quiet, we will stick our finger even deeper down her throat, and then we will throw the little missus out of the little window. The little missus will fall and break all of her little bones.

Little Lida was quiet and, terrified, she stared at the little old man in dread. And the little old man again stuck his face in Lidochka's little stomach. His prickly beard and mustache poked Lida.

Uncle Mika!

Uncle Mika! Lidochka whimpered quietly. At that moment there came a knock on the door.

Who's there? Uncle Mika asked in a stern voice, covering Little Lida's mouth.

Open the door! You have the girl! a woman's voice yelled from the other side of the door.

I have no one! Uncle Mika answered.

Little Lida freed up her mouth and was about to cry very loudly. Uncle Mika grabbed her by the throat and began to suffocate her.

Don't you dare! Not a peep! Uncle Mika said hoarsely.

Open the door! a man's voice issued from the corridor.

Later, this despicable old man was flogged and sent away. And Little Lida was returned to her papa and mama.

[*September 1935*]

Author's manuscript note: "I had decided to write something nasty and so I did, but I can't go on any further; it's far too despicable."

You see—he said—I have been watching . . .

You see—he said—I have been watching how for the third day you have been riding in a boat with them. One of them was sitting at the rudder, two rowed, and a fourth sat beside you and talked. I was standing awhile on the shore and watching how those two were rowing. Yes, I can state with certainty that they had in mind to kill you. The way they rowed was a sure sign of murderous intent. Rowing of that kind takes place only before a murder.

The lady wearing yellow gloves looked at Klopov.*

What does that mean? she said. What is so particular to rowing prior to a murder? Besides, what reason would they have to drown me?

Klopov turned toward the lady brusquely and said:

Do you know what a copper look is?

No, the lady said, instinctively moving away from Klopov.

Aha, said Klopov. When a fragile china cup falls from the dresser and flies downward, then at that moment, while it still flies through the air, you already know that it will make contact with the floor and shatter to pieces. Just so I know that if one person looks at another person with a copper look then, sooner or later, he will inevitably kill him.

They were looking at me with copper looks? the lady in the yellow gloves asked.

Yes, m'lady, Klopov said and put on his hat.

For quite some time they both remained silent.

Klopov sat with his head bowed down.

Forgive me, he suddenly said quietly.

* *Klopov*: literally, "Bedbugman."

The lady in yellow gloves looked at Klopov in surprise but remained silent.

This is all untrue, said Klopov. I invented the story of the copper look, just now, here. Sitting with you on the bench. You see, today I broke my watch and everything appears to me in a dark light.

Klopov removed from his pocket a handkerchief, unfolded it, and proffered to the lady his broken pocket watch.

I wore it for sixteen years. You understand what this means? To break a watch which for sixteen years has been ticking right here, below my heart? Do you own a watch?

[1935–36]

When the wife goes away . . .

When the wife goes away by herself somewhere, the husband races around the room and can't find a place to rest.

The husband's nails grow out appallingly, his head quivers, and his face breaks out in tiny black dots.

The neighbors console the husband left alone and ply him with jellied pork. But the lonely husband loses his appetite and survives on a diet consisting mostly of unsweetened tea.

By this time, his wife is bathing in a lake and accidentally snags her foot on an underwater root. A pike swims out from under the root and bites the wife on the heel. With a holler, the wife jumps out of the water and runs towards the house. The hostess's daughter runs out to meet the wife. The wife shows the hostess's daughter the wounded leg and asks her to bandage it.

In the evening, the wife writes the husband a letter detailing to him her misadventures.

The husband reads the letter and, becoming so overcome with concern, drops a glass of water, which falls to the floor and shatters.

The husband collects the shards of glass and cuts his hand on one of them.

Bandaging his wounded finger, the husband sits down and composes a letter to his wife. Then he goes out in the street to drop the letter in a mailbox.

But out in the street, the husband finds a cigarette box, and inside it, thirty thousand rubles.

The husband urgently writes his wife to come back, and they begin to live the good life.

[*1935–36*]

And now I will tell you about
how I was born ...

And now I will tell you about how I was born, how I was raised, and how the first signs of my genius were recognized. I was born twice. It happened in just this way:

My father married my mother in the year 1902, but my parents brought me into this world only at the end of the year 1905 because my father had wished that his child be born precisely on the New Year. Father had calculated that the impregnation must occur on the first of April and only on that day did he take a ride over to mother with the proposition that she become "with child."

The first time my father visited my mother's was on April 1 of the year 1903. Mother had long waited for this moment and was terribly overjoyed. But father, apparently, was in a very jovial mood and could not restrain himself and so said to mother: "April Fool's Day!"

Mother was terribly hurt and would not on that day allow father near her. And so we all had to wait until the following year.

In the year 1904, on the first of April, father again prepared to arrive at mother's with the same proposition. But mother, remembering the events of the previous year, said that now she no longer wished to be placed in such a preposterous position, and again would not let father near her. No matter how much father fumed, nothing helped.

And only a year hence did my father succeed in breaking down my mother's resolve and siring me.

And so my germination took place on the first of April in the year 1905.

However, all of father's plans were quashed, because I turned out to be premature and was born four months prior to term.

Father became so incensed that the neonatal nurse who delivered me, in her confusion, started to stuff me back in where I had just crawled out from.

One of our acquaintances who was present during the event, a student at the Military Medical Academy, declared that stuffing me back in would not work. Despite the student's warning, they stuffed me in, though, it should be noted, and as was later confirmed, stuff me in they did but, being in a rush, they managed to do it into the wrong place.

That's when the total pandemonium ensued.

The mother-to-be screams: "Give me my baby!" And they answer her: "Your baby is, so to speak, inside you." "How!" screams the expectant mother. "How could the newborn be inside me when I just gave birth to him!"

"But," they tell the mother-to-be, "perhaps you're mistaken?" "How!" screams mother, "Mistaken!? How can I be mistaken! I saw it with my own eyes; the baby was lying on the sheets just a moment ago!" "That is true," they tell her. "But, just, maybe, he crawled in somewhere." In a word, they themselves don't know what to tell the expectant mother.

And she continues to make a racket and demand her infant.

So they had to call in an experienced doctor. The experienced doctor looked the patient over and spread his arms in amazement, but soon figured it out and gave her a good dose of English salts. And so my mother had a massive movement, and I passed into this world a second time.

Then my father became incensed once again, because this, how can you, this so-called birth, that this isn't a human being yet but so to speak a partial delivery, and that it would perhaps be better to either stuff him back in or to put him away in an incubator.

And so they put me away in an incubator.

✦

I sat in the incubator for four months. I only remember that the incubator was made of glass, transparent and with a thermometer. I sat in the incubator on a wad of cotton. I don't remember anything else.

After four months they took me out of the incubator. They did so exactly on the first of January, 1906. In this way, I was born, sort of, a third time. And so, my birthday was counted precisely from January the first.

25 September of the year 1935

One personage, wringing
her hands in sorrow . . .

One personage, wringing her hands in sorrow, was saying, "What I need is an interest toward life, and not at all money. I am seeking enhancement not advancement. I need a husband, and not a rich man but a true talent, the director Meyerhold!"

September 28, 1935

A Fable

One man of limited stature said: "I am willing to accept anything, if I could only be a little taller." And just as he said this, he sees before him a good witch. And the man of limited stature stands there and out of fear is unable to say a word.

"Well?" the good witch says. And the man of limited stature stands there in silence. The good witch disappears. That's when the man of limited stature started to cry and chew his nails. First he bit off the nails on his hands, and then on his feet.

✦

Reader, consider this tale and you too will begin to feel very strange.

[*1935*]

The Carpenter Kushakov

Once upon a time there lived a carpenter. His name was Kushakov.

One time, he left his house to go to the corner store to buy some wood glue.

The thaw had begun and the street was very slippery.

The carpenter went several steps, slipped, fell, and split his forehead.

Akh!—the carpenter said, got up and went off in the direction of the pharmacy, got a bandage, and glued it on his forehead.

But as soon as he went out in the street and took several steps, he again slipped, fell, and split his nose.

Damn it!—the carpenter said and, going back to the pharmacy, bought himself a bandage and plastered it over his nose.

Then he again went out in the street, again slipped, fell, and split his face.

He had to go to the pharmacy once more to bandage his cheek.

You know what—the pharmacist told the carpenter. You fall and hurt yourself so often, I suggest you buy several bandages at once.

No—said the carpenter—I won't fall again!

But when he went out in the street, he again slipped, fell, and split his chin.

Rotten black ice!—the carpenter screamed and ran off again to the pharmacy.

You see—the pharmacist said. So you did fall again.

No!—the carpenter yelled. I don't want to hear about it! Just give me a bandage, quick!

The pharmacist sold him the bandage, he put it on and ran for home.

But at home they didn't recognize him and wouldn't let him inside the apartment.

I am the carpenter Kushakov! the carpenter screamed.

You don't say!—they replied from inside, bolting the door shut and putting it on the chain.

The carpenter Kushakov stood around for a while on the stairs, spat, and went out in the street.

[*1935*]

There once lived a man,
and his name was Kuznetsov . . .

There once lived a man, and his name was Kuznetsov.*

Once upon a time, his footstool broke. And he went out of his house to go to the store, to buy wood glue, to fix the footstool.

As Kuznetsov was passing a house under construction, a brick fell from above and hit Kuznetsov on the head.

Kuznetsov collapsed but immediately got up and felt his head. A huge bump had erupted on it.

Kuznetsov stroked the bump with his hand and said:

I, citizen Kuznetsov, left my house and went to the store to . . . so as to . . . in order to . . . Akh, what is going on! I forgot what I was going to the store for!

At this very moment, a second brick fell off the roof, again knocking Kuznetsov on the head.

Ahhh! Kuznetsov screamed, grabbed his head, and felt a second bump popping up. What a tale! I, citizen Kuznetsov, left my house and went . . . and set off for . . . and proceeded to . . . now, where is it that I was going? I forgot where I was going!

Just then, a third brick fell on Kuznetsov from above. And a third bump erupted on Kuznetsov's head.

Ouch, ouch, ouch! Kuznetsov screamed, grabbing ahold of his head. I, citizen Kuznetsov left . . . I went out from . . . I departed . . . I came out of a cellar? No. I climbed out of a barrel? No! Where was it I left from?

From the roof tumbled a fourth brick, which struck Kuznetsov on the back of the head, and on the back of his head rose a fourth bump.

* *Kuznetsov*: literally, "Cricketman."

Well, oh well! Kuznetsov said, scratching the back of his head. I . . . I . . . I . . . So who am I? Did I somehow forget my name? What a doozy! What is it I am called? Vasily Cockerman? No. Nikolai Bootsoff? Pantelei Lynxter? No. Well, who am I?

But just then a fifth brick fell off the roof and struck Kuznetsov on the back of his head so hard that Kuznetsov once and for all forgot everything in the world and, having screamed "Ahhh! Ahhh!" ran off down the alley.

November 1, 1935

So, my sweet little Lena . . .

So, my sweet little Lena—her aunt said—I am leaving and you stay home and be a smart little girl: don't drag the cat around by the tail, don't pour farina into the table clock, don't swing on the ceiling lamp, and don't drink the toxic ink. Good?

Good—said little Lena, picking up the large scissors.

Very well—said the aunt—I'll return in about two hours and bring you some mints. Do you want some mint candies?

I want—said little Lena, holding in one hand the big scissors and picking up with her other hand a cloth napkin from the table.

Alright, I'll see you soon, dear little Lena—the aunt said, and went out.

I'll see you! I'll see you!—little Lena sang, inspecting the napkin.

The aunt had already left, and little Lena continued the whole time to hum the tune.

I'll see you! I'll see you!—sang little Lena—I'll see you, auntie! I'll see you, four-cornered napkin! With these words Lena began working the scissors.

And now, and now—little Lena sang—the napkin has become round! And now, a half circle! And now it is small! It was one napkin, and now there are many little napkins!

Lenochka gazed at the tablecloth.

And this tablecloth is also now one! sang Lenochka. And now there will be two of them! And now there are two tablecloths! And now three! One bigger and two smaller! And this table is only one!

Lenochka ran to the kitchen and returned with an ax.

And now from one table we will make two! sang Lenochka and struck the table with the ax. But no matter how long Lenochka labored, she only managed to split off a few chips.

[*1935*]

The Brave Hedgehog

On the table there stood a box.

The animals approached the box and started to examine, smell, and lick it.

And the box suddenly—one, two, three—popped open.

And from the box—one, two, three—popped out a snake.

The animals got scared and ran off.

Only the hedgehog didn't get scared and yelled: "Kukareku!"

No, not that way! The hedgehog yelled: "Af-afaf!"

No, and not that way! The hedgehog yelled: "Meow-meow-meow!"

No, again not like that! I myself don't know how.

Who knows, how do hedgehogs scream?

[*1935*]

From the Notebooks (mid-1930s)

They're saying that all broads will soon have their buttocks cut off and be let out for a walk along Volodarsky Prospect.

This is untrue! No broads will have their buttocks cut off.

———

A man with a stupid face ate an apricot, burped, and died. The waiters carried him out into the corridor leading to the kitchen, placed him on the floor along the wall, and covered him with a dirty tablecloth.

———

One man, from his early youth into his deep old age, always slept on his back, with his arms crossed on his chest. And finally one day he died. The moral—always sleep on your side.

———

He speaks in six known and six unknown languages.

The Fate of the Professor's Wife

One time, a certain professor ate something that didn't agree with him, and he started to vomit.

His wife came over and said:

What's with you?

And the professor says:

Nothing.

So the wife left again.

The professor lay down on the ottoman. He lay there for a while, rested up, and went off to his job.

And at work, a surprise awaited him; they've shrunk his salary: from 650, they've left him with only 500 rubles.

The professor tried this and that—but it was no use. The professor went to see the director, and the director showed him the door. He went to the accountant and the accountant said:

Talk to the director.

So the professor got on a train and set off for Moscow.

On the way, the professor came down with the flu. He got to Moscow and couldn't even get off the train unaided.

They put the professor on a stretcher and took him to the hospital.

The professor lay in the hospital less than four days and died.

They burned the professor's body in the crematorium, placed the ashes in a little jar, and sent them off to his wife. So the professor's wife was sitting there, drinking her coffee.

Suddenly the doorbell rang. What's this?

There's a package for you.

The wife, rejoicing and grinning from ear to ear, stuffed a half-ruble coin in the mailman's hand, and quickly unwrapped the package.

She looked and saw inside was a little jar of ashes with a note: "This is all that remains of your spouse."

The wife got very upset, cried for close to three hours, and then went off to bury the little jar of ashes. She wrapped the jar in a newspaper and carried it to the Park of the First Five Year Plan, formerly known as the Tavrichesky.

The professor's wife had picked out a more secluded alley and just as she was about to bury the jar, here comes the watchman.

Hey! the guard yelled, What are you doing here?

The professor's wife got scared and said:

I just wanted to trap some frogs in this little jar.

Well, the guard said, that's alright with me, but just keep in mind: walking on the grass is strictly prohibited.

When the watchman left, the professor's wife buried the little jar in the ground, stomped the earth around it flat, and went off for a walk in the park.

But in the park, some sailor kept pestering her.

Come with me, let's go—he says—let's go and sleep together.

She says:

Why sleep when it is daytime?

And he just keeps repeating: sleep this, sleep that. And indeed, the professor's wife becomes very drowsy.

She's walking down the street and falling asleep.

Racing around her are some strange people, blue ones, green ones, and all she wants to do is go to sleep. She's walking in her sleep. And she dreams a dream: it seems Leo Tolstoy is walking towards her with a chamber pot in his hands. She asks him, "What's the meaning of this?"

And he gestures with his finger at the chamber pot, and says:

Well—he says—I have made something here, and now I'm carrying it off for the entire world to see. Let everyone—he says—look at it.

The professor's wife also starts to take a closer look and she sees, it seems, that it is no longer Leo Tolstoy but a barn, and inside the barn sits a laying hen.

The professor's wife started trying to catch the chicken, but the chicken scuttled under the couch and was peeking out from underneath it, only now as a rabbit.

The professor's wife started crawling under the couch after the rabbit and woke up.

She looks around: and indeed, she is lying under the couch.

The professor's wife climbs out from under the couch, and sees—it is indeed her room. And there's the table with the unfinished coffee. On the table is a note: "This is all that remains of your spouse."

The professor's wife started crying again and sat down to finish her coffee.

Suddenly the doorbell rings. What's this?

We're going for a ride.

Where? the professor's wife asks.

To the madhouse, the strange people say.

The professor's wife started screaming and resisting, but the people grabbed her and drove her off to the insane asylum.

And so, sitting there on a bunk bed in the madhouse is an entirely normal professor's wife, with a fishing rod in her hands, trying to catch some sort of invisible fish swimming around on the floor.

This professor's wife is but one sad example of how many unfortunates there are in life who occupy a position other than the one that was intended for them.

August 21, 1936

What Happened to Petrakov

So, one time Petrakov wanted to go to sleep, but he missed the bed and landed on the floor so hard that he was lying there on the floor and couldn't get up.

And so, Petrakov gathered up all of his remaining strength and raised himself up on his knees. But his strength gave out, and he again collapsed on his belly and just lay there.

Petrakov lay on the floor a full five hours. First he just lay there, but then he fell asleep.

Sleep replenished Petrakov's energy, and he woke up completely refreshed.

He got up, walked across the room, and carefully got into his bed.

"Well," he thought, "now I can get some sleep." But he was really not sleepy anymore. He tossed and turned from side to side but there was no way he was going to fall back asleep again.

So that, in a nutshell, is about it.

August 21, 1936

An Occurrence

Once upon a time, Eagleman stuffed himself with roasted peas and croaked. And Winger, learning of this, also croaked. And Spiridonov croaked all by himself. And Spiridonov's wife fell off her high chair and also croaked. And Spiridonov's children drowned in a pond. And Spiridonov's mother turned into an alky and became homeless. And Mikhailov stopped grooming himself and came down with scurvy. And Circleman drew a lady with a whip in her hands and went mad. And Crosseshimself received, via the telegraph, four hundred rubles and got so high-and-mighty that he was removed from his post.

Nice, decent people simply don't know how to place themselves on good footing.

August 22, 1936

A certain mechanic decided
to stand at work . . .

A certain mechanic decided to stand at work, by turn first on one leg, then on the other leg, so as not to tire as much.

But nothing came of this, and he began to tire more than he had before and his work did not flow as smoothly as it had earlier.

The mechanic was called into the manager's office and issued a written reprimand.

But the mechanic decided he would struggle to overcome his natural inclination to stand on both legs and continued to stand over his work on one leg.

The mechanic wrestled with himself for quite some time and, finally, having felt a twinge in his lower back, which got worse with each passing day, was forced to seek help from a doctor.

August 27, 1936

The Cashier Woman

Masha found a mushroom, picked it, and took it off to the market. At the market, they hit Masha on the head and even threatened to kick her in the shins. Masha got scared and ran off.

Masha ran into the co-op store, trying to hide there, behind the cash register. And the manager sees Masha and says:

What is that in your hands?

And Masha says:

A mushroom.

And the manager says:

Boy, you're a lively one! You want me to give you a job?

And Masha says:

No you won't.

You'll see, I will too! And so he did, and he gave her the run of the till.

Masha spun the knobs this way and that and suddenly died.

The police came, made out a report, and required the manager to pay a fine of fifteen rubles.

The manager said:

What am I being fined for?

And the police said:

Murder.

The manager, getting scared, rushed to pay the fine, and said:

Just hurry up and take this dead cashier woman away.

And the counter lady from the fruit department said:

No, it's not true, she wasn't the cashier. She was just pressing the buttons on the register. And the cashier is sitting over there.

The police said:

We don't care: we were asked to take the cashier away, so we're taking her away.

The police started moving toward the cashier lady.

The cashier lady lay down on the floor behind the register and said:

I won't go.

The police said:

Why won't you go, you foolish woman?

The cashier lady said:

You'll bury me alive.

The police started lifting her up off the floor, but couldn't quite manage to do it, because the cashier lady was so portly.

You have to grab her by the feet, said the counter lady from the fruit department.

No, said the manager, I use this cashier lady for a wife, so I ask you to please not expose her down under there.

The cashier lady said:

Did you hear that? Don't you dare expose me down under there.

The police grabbed the cashier lady by her underarms and dragged her out of the premises.

The manager ordered the sales staff to clean up the store and re-open for business.

So what are we going to do with this dead girl? said the counter lady from the fruit department, pointing at Masha.

Oh, Lordy, said the manager. We really did make a mess of things! Yes, indeed, what are we going to do with the dead girl?

And who will sit behind the cash register? asked one of the sales ladies.

The manager grabbed his head with his hands, scattered the apples on the floor with his knee, and said:

What a rigmarole this has become!

Rigmarole, the sales staff said in a chorus.

Then the manager scratched his mustache and said:

Ha-ha! You won't back me into a corner so easily! We'll put the dead girl behind the register, and the customers just might not figure out who's sitting behind there.

They put the dead girl back behind the cash register, placed a cigarette between her teeth, so that she bore a better resemblance to a living person, and stuck the mushroom in her hand, for greater effect.

The dead girl was sitting behind the register, as though alive, only the color of her face was quite green, and one eye was bulging open, while the other was tightly shut.

Not bad, the manager said. It will do.

And the customers are already beating down the door, anxious to get in. Why aren't they opening up the cooperative? One housewife wearing a silk cape in particular was raising a racket, shaking her purse, banging the heel of the shoe in her hand on the door handle. And behind the housewife was some old lady with a pillowcase on her head, yelling and cursing and calling the store manager a lousy hoarder.

The manager unlocked the door and let the crowd in. All the customers immediately made a dash for the meat department, and then over to where they sold sugar and pepper. And the old lady headed straight for the fish department, but on her way there, caught sight of the cashier girl and stopped dead in her tracks.

Good Lord, she said, may the Holy One protect us!

The housewife in the silk cape had already visited all the departments and was racing toward the cash register. But as soon as she catches sight of the cashier girl, she stops dead in her tracks and just stands there, staring in silence. And the sales staff are also silent, looking over at the manager. And the manager peeks out from behind the counter, waiting to see what will happen next.

The housewife in the silk cape turns to the sales ladies and says:

Who's that you got sitting behind the cash register?

And the sales staff all remains silent, not knowing how to answer.

And the manager is also mum.

And then the crowd rushes in from all sides. They'd already assembled out in the street. The street sweepers had all come out. The policemen were blowing their whistles. In a word, a genuine scandal.

The crowd would have kept at it into the night, but somebody had mentioned that in Lake Alley, there were old women falling out of windows. So that was when the crowd around the co-op thinned out, because some of them had moved over to Lake Alley.

August 31, 1936

Father and Daughter

Natasha had two pieces of candy. Then she ate one of the candies and had one piece left. Natasha placed the remaining piece of candy on the table in front of herself and started crying.

Suddenly, she sees that there are two pieces of candy again on the table in front of her.

Natasha ate one of the candies and again started to cry.

Natasha is crying, but at the same time she is peeking with one eye at the table, to see if a second piece of candy has reappeared. But the second candy hadn't reappeared.

Natasha stopped crying and started singing.

She sang and sang and suddenly she died.

Natasha's father came and carried her down to the building super's.

Look here, Natasha's father says, I need you to bear witness to her death.

The super blew on a rubber stamp and affixed it to Natasha's forehead.

Thank you, said Natasha's father, and carried her off to the cemetery.

The watchman at the cemetery, a certain Matvei, sat at all times by the gates and would not let anyone enter the cemetery, so that they all had to bury the bodies right there in the street.

Natasha's father buried her in the street, took off his hat, placed it on the ground over where he had dug the grave, and went back home.

He returned home, and Natasha is already sitting there.

How could this be? Very simple: she climbed out of the grave and ran home.

What a thing! The father got so flummoxed that he collapsed and died.

Natasha calls the super to come and says to him:

Please bear witness to his death.

The super blew on the rubber stamp and affixed it to a piece of paper, and then on the same piece of paper wrote: "The following attests that such and such did indeed die."

Natasha picked up the piece of paper and carried it off to the cemetery for the burial. And the watchman Matvei tells her:

No way am I going to let you in.

Natasha says:

But I only wish to bury this little piece of paper.

And the watchman says:

Don't even bother asking me.

Natasha buried the little piece of paper in the street, put her thin little socks over the place where she had buried the paper and went home.

She returns home, and her father is already sitting there, playing against himself on the toy billiard table with the little metal balls.

Natasha was so surprised, but she didn't say anything and went to her room, to grow.

She grew and grew, and in four years transformed into a beautiful young lady. And Natasha's father grew old and bent over. But both of them, as soon as they recall how they had confused each other for dead folks, they fall over on the couch and start to chuckle. They laugh so hard, sometimes for an entire twenty minutes.

And the neighbors, as soon as they hear their laughter, immediately get dressed up and go out to the movies. And one time, they went off like that and never came back. Got run over by an automobile, I think.

September 1, 1936

One time, Petya Nailor was pacing around the apartment . . .

One time, Petya Nailor was pacing around the apartment. He was dying of boredom. He picked up from the floor a piece of paper that the maid had dropped. The paper turned out to be a torn newspaper. This was not interesting. Petya tried to catch the cat, but the cat hid under the dresser. Petya went into the foyer to get an umbrella so that he could dislodge the cat with it. But by the time Petya returned, the cat had disappeared. Petya searched for the cat under the sofa and behind the trunk, but the cat was nowhere to be found. However, instead, behind the trunk Petya found a hammer. Petya picked up the hammer and started thinking of something interesting to do with it. Petya used the hammer to bang on the floor, but this too was boring. That's when Petya remembered that on the chair in the foyer was a full box of nails. Petya went to the entrance hall, selected from the box several nails, the longer ones, and started thinking about what he could drive them into. If the cat were around then of course it would be interesting to hammer it with one nail by the ear to the door and with another by the tail into the threshold. But the cat had vanished. Petya saw the grand piano. And so, Petya walked up to it and hammered three of the longest nails into the lid of the grand piano.

October 9, 1936

Kulakov squeezed himself into a deep armchair . . .

Kulakov* squeezed himself into a deep armchair and immediately fell asleep. He fell asleep sitting up and several hours later woke up lying in a coffin. Kulakov realized right away that he was lying in a coffin and was seized by a paralyzing terror. With his clouded-over eyes, he looked around, and everywhere, in every direction he could cast his gaze, he saw only flowers: flowers in baskets, bouquets of flowers wrapped in ribbons, wreaths of flowers, and flowers scattered about separately.

"I am being buried," Kulakov thought to himself, filling with horror, but suddenly he felt a sense of pride, that he, such an insignificant person, was being buried with so much pomp, and with such a great quantity of flowers.

[*1936*]

---

* Literally, "Fistman"; also Soviet speak for affluent peasants who were the target of Stalin's collectivization campaign.

One man went to sleep with faith . . .

One man went to sleep with faith, and woke up faithless.

As luck would have it, in this man's room stood very precise medical scales, and the man was in the habit of weighing himself daily, every morning and every night.

And so, before going to bed the previous evening, having weighed himself, the man determined that he weighed four stone and twenty-one pounds. And on the next morning, having woken up without faith, the man weighed himself again and determined that he now weighed only four stone and thirteen pounds. "It may thus be determined," the man concluded, "that my faith had weighed approximately eight pounds."

[*1936–37*]

Two men got to talking . . .

Two men got to talking. As they were speaking, one of them was stammering on the consonants, and the other one on both the consonants and the vowels.

It was nice when they finally stopped talking—as though the hissing of a gas stove had been turned off.

[*1936–37*]

The Rat

"M'yes!" I said once again with my voice quaking. The rat nodded its head in the other direction but continued looking at me just the same.

"What do you want from me?" I said in despair.

"Nothing!" the rat suddenly announced loud and clear. This was so unexpected that all the signs of my fear had somehow seemed to vanish. And the rat, wandering off to one side of the room, sat down on the floor by the oven.

"I like the warmth," the rat said. "In our basement, it is so terribly cold."

[before January 1937]

I detest children . . .

I detest children, old men, old crones, and elderly wise people.

Poisoning children is cruel. But something needs to be done about them!

I find only young and healthy plump women endearing. To the other representatives of humanity I relate with nothing but mistrust.

Old women, who carry around wise thoughts in their heads, should be caught in leg traps.

Every mug bearing an intelligent expression calls forth in me a very unpleasant sensation.

What are flowers anyway? Any woman between her legs smells a whole lot better. Both one and the other are natural; that is why no one will dare take exception with my words.

[*second half of 1930s*]

From "The Blue Notebook" [No. 10]

There once lived a redheaded man who had no eyes and no ears. He didn't even have any hair so that he was called a redhead only provisionally, as a figure of speech.

He was unable to speak because he didn't have a mouth. And he also didn't have a nose.

He didn't have hands and he didn't have legs.

And he had no stomach, no back, no spine, and no innards to speak of, either. He didn't have anything! In fact, it's impossible to understand who it is we're talking about here. I think it would be better if we change the subject now.

January 7, 1937

A certain man, who no longer wished to eat split peas . . .

A certain man, who no longer wished to eat split peas, set out for a large food market in order to find something different for himself, perhaps some seafood, deli meats, or perhaps even dairy.

In the deli meats department there was much that was interesting, and there was of course ham. But the ham cost eighteen rubles, and this was too rich for him. Right for his pocket was a bologna, red in color with darkish gray spots. But this bologna for some reason smelled like cheese so that even the salesman himself said that he wouldn't recommend it.

In the fish department there was nothing, because the fish department temporarily moved where the wine department had been, and the wine department where the deli had been, and the deli department where the dairy had been, and in the dairy department there stood a manager with such a huge nose that the customers were huddling under the arch, too afraid to approach any nearer to the counter.

And so this man jostled his way around the store for a bit and exited onto the street. The person whom I have been speaking of was not distinguishable by any particular qualities deserving of a separate description. He was moderately thin, moderately poor, and moderately lazy. I can't even remember how he was dressed. I can only recall that he wore something brown, perhaps pants, perhaps a jacket, or perhaps it was only a brown tie. I think his name was Ivan Yakovlevich.

Ivan Yakovlevich exited the food market and headed for home. Having returned home, Ivan Yakovlevich took off his hat, sat down on the couch, and rolled himself a cigarette out of loose tobacco, stuck it in a holder, lit it with a match, smoked it, rolled a second cigarette, lit it, got up, put on his hat, and walked out onto the street.

He was bored with his small, insignificant life, and so he set off in the direction of the Hermitage.

Having reached the Fontanka, Ivan Yakovlevich stopped in his tracks as though wishing to turn back, but suddenly he became ashamed before the people passing by: God forbid they would start looking over and measuring him up and down, for here's a man, walking, and then he suddenly turns around and starts walking in the opposite direction. Pedestrians always pay attention to these sorts of things.

Ivan Yakovlevich stood on the corner, across from the pharmacy. And to resolve the confusion of the passersby about his situation, Ivan Yakovlevich pretended, acting as though he was looking for a street address.

Without ceasing to look at the building, he took several strides along the Fontanka, then retraced his steps, without understanding himself why, and entered the pharmacy.

The pharmacy was packed with people. Ivan Yakovlevich tried to squeeze through to the counter, but he was pushed aside. He then looked over at the glass display case in which, standing in different poses, stood assorted flasks of various perfumes and eaux de cologne.

It is not worth describing what else Ivan Yakovlevich did, because all of his affairs were far too minor and insignificant. It is only important to note that he never did make it to the Hermitage that day and, towards six o'clock, he returned home.

At home he smoked four hand-rolled cigarettes in a row and then lay down on the couch, turned to face the wall, and tried to fall asleep.

But apparently, Ivan Yakovlevich had had too much to smoke, because his heart was beating very rapidly, and sleep evaded him.

Ivan Yakovlevich sat up on the couch and dangled his feet to the floor.

He sat in this position until half past eight o'clock.

What I should do is fall in love with a beautiful young lady, Ivan Yakovlevich said, and he immediately covered his mouth with his hand and bugged his eyes out.

With a young brunette, said Ivan Yakovlevich, moving the hand away from his mouth. The one I saw today in the street.

Ivan Yakovlevich rolled a cigarette and lit it. Three rings resounded in the corridor.

It's for me, said Ivan Yakovlevich, continuing to sit still on the sofa.

January 13, 1937

Trunk (A Hard Case)

A man with a thin neck clambers into a large piece of luggage and, closing the lid behind himself, begins to asphyxiate himself. Here I am, struggling for air, the man with the thin neck says. In a foot-locker, struggling for air because I have a thin neck. The top of the case is shut and will not admit a whiff. And so, I will struggle for air but in no case open the top. I will thus become witness to the struggle between life and death. The battle will be staged, artificial; the odds even, because in reality death always triumphs; but life condemned to death can only wrestle the enemy conscientiously until the last breath without losing otherwise useless hope. In this very struggle which will now proceed, life will become aware of its means of victory; it will have to convince my hands to pry open the top. We'll see who gets whom! It's only unfortunate how bad this place stinks of mothballs. If life wins out, from now on I will pack my things in tobacco leaves . . . Here it comes. I can't breathe any longer. I'm dead; that's certain. There will be no saving me! And nothing elevated stirs in my head. I'm dying!

Oy! What's this? Something's happening but I can't understand exactly what. I saw or heard something.

Oy! There it goes again. My God! I can't breathe. I am dying, I think . . .

What is going on? Why do I sing? It seems that my neck is hurting . . . And where is the trunk? How am I seeing all these things in my room? And how come I'm lying on the floor? Where is the case?

The man with the thin neck pulls himself off the floor and looks around. No trunk in sight anywhere. On top of the chairs and on the bed, all the stuff the chest had contained has been spread out, but the trunk itself has vanished.

The man with the thin neck says: Thus does life overcome death, by means to me imponderable.

January 30, 1937

Ivan Andreevich Turnip

Ivan Andreevich Turnip was born precisely fifty-six years ago. He is such a well-known personality now that there's really no need for me to tell you exactly who he is. Just to think how much he has managed to accomplish in only his fifty-six years. Yes, a genius is not some shank—you can't hide him in a sack.

Realizing that it was his birthday, Ivan Andreevich Turnip went out and bought a can of sardines and hid it inside the drawer of his writing table.

I am just too famous to count on no one showing up to congratulate me, said Turnip to himself. This way, if someone comes, I will treat them to sardines.

Turnip sat down on the sofa bed and began to wait.

At eight o'clock in the evening, the doorbell rang out and he raced across the room to open it. But having run down the corridor past the bathroom he understood that he was going the wrong way so he turned around and headed towards the foyer. But, having reached the foyer, he couldn't understand what it was he was doing there and, slowly dragging his feet, he ambled back to his room.

[*1935–37*]

Tumbling Babushkas (Excessive Curiosity)

A babushka, out of an excess of curiosity, slipped and spilled out of a window and splattered herself. Another babushka stuck her head out of a window to stare down at this splattered one but, from an excess of curiosity, also plunged out and, tumbling down, also got splattered.

Later, from a window fell a third babushka, then a fourth and a fifth one.

By the time the sixth babushka came flying out, I was bored with this spectacle and took a walk to the Marlutsky Market where they say some blind cripple was given a hand-knitted shawl.

[*1936–37*]

Connection

Philosopher!

1

I am writing you this letter in reply to your letter, which you are planning to write to me in reply to my letter, that I have written to you.

2

A certain violinist bought himself a magnet and carried it home. On his way home, he was set upon by a group of hooligans who knocked his hat off. The wind picked up the hat and carried it down the street.

3

The violinist put the magnet down on the ground and started running after his hat. The hat fell into a puddle of nitric acid and decomposed there.

4

Meanwhile, the hooligans grabbed the magnet and made tracks with it.

5

The violinist returned home without his hat and coat, because the hat decomposed in nitric acid, and the violinist, upset by the loss of his hat, forgot his coat on the streetcar.

6

The conductor of this streetcar brought the coat to a rag shop and traded it in for some sour cream, grain, and tomatoes.

7

The conductor's father-in-law stuffed himself with the tomatoes and died. They put the conductor's father-in-law's corpse in the morgue, but then they confused him with another and in place of the conductor's father-in-law buried some old woman.

8

On the old woman's grave, they placed a white marker with the inscription: "Anton Sergeevich Kondratev."

9

After eleven years, this marker was eaten through by worms, and it collapsed. And the cemetery watchman sawed this marker in four and burned it in his stove. And on this fire, the cemetery watchman's wife made soup out of a cauliflower.

10

But when the soup was good and ready, a fly dropped from the wall and fell right into this soup. They gave the soup away to the pauper Timofeus.

11

The pauper Timofeus ate the soup and told the pauper Nikolai about the cemetery watchman's generosity.

12

On the next day, the pauper Nikolai came to the cemetery watchman's and started begging alms. But the cemetery watchman gave Nikolai nothing and instead chased him away.

13

The pauper Nikolai became so incensed that he set fire to the cemetery watchman's house.

14

The fire jumped from the house to the church, and the church burned down.

15

A long investigation ensued, but the cause of the fire was never established.

16

In the place where the church had been, they built a club and on the day of the grand opening they gave a concert, at which the violinist performed, the one that fourteen years ago had lost his coat.

17

Among the audience sat the son of one of those hooligans, who fourteen years ago had knocked the hat off this violinist's head.

18

After the concert, they went home in the same streetcar. But in the streetcar that was following them, the driver was that same conductor who had once sold the violinist's coat at the rag shop.

19

And so they are riding late in the evening across the city: in front, the violinist and the son of the hooligan, and behind them, the streetcar driver and former conductor.

20

They are riding without being aware of the connections between them, nor will they ever, until their dying day, find these out.

September 14, 1937

The Four-Legged Crow

Once upon a time there lived a four-legged crow. Truth be told, she had five feet, but there's no point in talking about that.

So once upon a time the four-legged crow bought herself some coffee and thought: "So here I am, got myself some coffee, but what to do with it?"

And then, as bad luck would have it, a fox came trotting by. She saw the crow and yelled to her:

"Hey!" she yells. "You, crow!"

And the crow yells back at the fox:

"You're a crow yourself!"

And the fox yells at the crow:

"And you, crow, are a pig!"

That's when the crow, being upset, spilled her coffee. And the fox scrammed. And the crow climbed down to the ground and slunk off on all four or, more precisely, all five of her feet to her despicable house.

February 13, 1938

How One Man Fell to Pieces

They say that all the good broads are fat-bottomed. Oh well; I love the big-breasted ladies, I like how they smell—having said this, he began to increase in size until, reaching the ceiling, he crumbled into a thousand tiny pellets.

The janitor Pantalei came in and swept these balls into a dustpan, the one he usually used to collect horse manure, and then he carried them off somewhere, to the back of the yard.

And the sun shone on as before, and the pneumatic ladies continued smelling as delightful as ever.

August 23, 1938

Selected Prose from the Late Years

✦ 1938–1941 ✦

NKVD Confession (1931)

The significance of this signed confession, certainly produced under se-
vere duress, emerges in light of the seeming absurdity of its context and
full implication, being the equivalent of signing one's own commuted
death sentence. The naming of names, otherwise abhorrent, suggests
that those named had already been implicated, reflecting perhaps
the commonly held belief that implicating as many people as possible
made their actual execution physically impossible, as well as the sheer
powerlessness of the situation. The poignancy of the absurdity, that the
composition of children's poetry might constitute "anti-revolutionary"
activity, points to the surreal, nightmarish quality of Soviet reality
that Kharms's late work singularly expresses. (Though bearing a re-
semblance, the Kalashnikov implicated here was not the later-to-be
revered weapons designer, who incidentally happened to have been a
life-long composer of poems.)

Embarking on the path of a sincere confession, I testify that I acted
as the ideologue of an anti-Soviet group of writers working primar-
ily in the sphere of children's literature, which, besides me, included
A. Vvedensky, Bakhterev, Razumovsky, Vladimirov (deceased), and,
somewhat earlier, Zabolotsky and K. Vaginov. The creative work of
our group can be divided into two parts. These were, in the first place,
"trans-sense," essentially counter-revolutionary poems intended by
us for adults, which, by virtue of their content and tendency, could
not be published under contemporary Soviet conditions, and which
we disseminated among the anti-Soviet intelligentsia to whom we
were connected by shared political convictions. The dissemination

Daniil Kharms, *I Am a Phenomenon Quite Out of the Ordinary*, trans. Anthony Anem-
one and Peter Scotto (Boston: Academic Studies Press, 2013), 293–94.

of this aforementioned portion of our creative work was conducted by means of the reproduction of our literary works on typewriters and the distribution of these works in manuscript form, through scandalous readings of them at various anti-Soviet salons, in particular at the apartment of P. P. Kalashnikov, a man disposed to monarchist views whose apartment systematically served as a gathering place for people with anti-Soviet opinions. Besides which, we also participated in public readings of our works for adults for wider audiences, for example, at the Press House and the University, where the student audience at our last reading responded with extraordinary vehemence, demanding that we be sent to Solovki camps and calling us counter-revolutionaries. The second part of our creative work relates to the sphere of children's literature. We considered our work for children, as opposed to those for adults, inauthentic, intended simply to earn us the material wherewithal for existence. By virtue of our political convictions and literary platform, we consciously introduced ideas politically hostile to Soviet reality into the sphere of children's literature, and did harm to the cause of the Soviet formation of the rising generation. Our "trans-sense" language is antithetical to the materialist purposes of Soviet artistic literature, it being based completely on a mystical and idealistic philosophy, and is counter-revolutionary under the present conditions.

I admit that, as the head of the aforementioned group of writers of children's literature, I engaged in anti-Soviet activity. In my future depositions I will detail and expand upon this protocol.

Daniil Kharms
December 18, 1931

From the Diaries (1937–1938)

June 1, 1937. 2 hours 40 minutes.

An even more terrifying time has arrived for me. At the Children's Literature publishing house, they are up in arms about one of my poems and have begun to bait and persecute me. They have stopped publishing me, explaining it away with "We can't pay you because of some technical error." My sense is that something mysterious and evil is taking place behind the scenes. We have nothing to eat. We go unbearably hungry.

I know the end has come. I am now going off to visit ChildLit to receive a refusal of my request for payment.

June 18, 1937. In Ilya's room.

I've been struck completely dumb. This is terrifying. Complete impotence, in every sense of the word. The unsteadiness is even evident in my handwriting.

But what insane persistence I have towards my vice. I am able to stick with it for hours, day in and day out, in order to accomplish my thing; I am unable to, yet still stick with it for hours. This is the meaning of passionate interest!

Enough with pretensions: I have no interest in anything else, except in this.

Inspiration and interest are one and the same thing.

Evading a divine inspiration is just as difficult as escaping a vice. When you're infused with divine inspiration, everything else vanishes and only this one thing remains.

That is why a vice is, in its own way, a sort of inspiration.

A genuine interest is the most important thing in our lives.

A person deprived of an interest for absolutely anything perishes quickly.

An excessively one-sided and powerful lust overwhelmingly increases the intensity of a human life; just one more nudge, and the person goes bonkers.

A person is incapable of fulfilling his gift if he is not guided in this by his genuine interest.

If a person's genuine interest coincides with the thrust of his gift, then such a person achieves greatness.

November 16, 1937

I no longer wish to live. I have no need of anything: not a shred of hope left. I have not a prayer for the Lord, let His will be done, whatever He intends for me, be it death or be it life—whatever He intends. Into thine hands, oh, Lord, Jesus Christ, I commit my spirit. Keep me from harm, have mercy on me, and grant me eternal life. Amen.

Daniil Kharms

———

I don't have the strength to do anything. I don't want to live.

January 12, 1938

I am amazed by human perseverance. It is already January 12, 1938. Our situation has become even more desperate, but we're still scraping by. Dear Lord, please send us a prompt and easy death.

———

How low I have fallen; few have fallen this low. One thing is certain: as low as I've fallen, there is no getting up.

March 20, 1938

Came to the window naked. In the house across the street someone must have taken an exception, the sailor's widow, I think. A policeman came barging in, with the yard sweeper, and someone else in tow. They declared that I have been disturbing the neighbors across the street from me for over three years already. So I have hung some curtains. What is more appealing to the eye, an old woman wearing nothing but a chemise or a young man, buck-naked? And for whom is it less acceptable to show themselves au naturel?

March 25, 1938

Our state of affairs has gotten even worse. I don't know what we will eat today. And how we are going to eat at all in the future—I haven't the faintest idea.

We are starving.

April 9, 1938

I'm at my wit's end. Yesterday, I spoke with Andreev. Our conversation was quite desperate. No hope left. We are starving. Marina is getting weaker, and I have a terrible toothache to boot.

We are perishing—God help us!

May 26 [1938]

Marina stays in bed all day in a foul mood. I love her so very much, but how harrowing it is to be married.

I am tormented by my "sex." For weeks, and sometimes months, I have not known a woman.

1. There is one purpose to every human life: immortality.
1a. There is one purpose to every human life: achieving immortality.
2. One pursues immortality by continuing his bloodline, another by accomplishing great mortal deeds in order to immortalize one's name. And only the third leads a righteous and holy life in order to achieve immortality as life eternal.
3. A man has but two interests: the mundane—food, drink, warmth, women, and rest; and the celestial—immortality.
4. All that is earthly is a confirmation of death.
5. There is one straight line upon which all that is mortal lies. And only that which is not plotted on this axis may serve as confirmation of eternity.
6. And for this reason man seeks a deviation from this earthly road and considers it beautiful or brilliant.

June 9, 1938

Marishenka left me and has settled in, for now, at Varvara Sergeevna's.*

———

I despise people who are capable of speaking for more than seven minutes in a row. There is nothing more tedious in this world than somebody retelling you their dream, or how they fought in the war, or about their trip to the south.

Long-windedness is the mother of mediocrity!

* Kharms's aunt.

I raised the dust . . .

I raised the dust. Children were running after me, tearing the clothes on their bodies. Old men and women were falling off roofs. I was whistling, I was thundering, I was gnashing my teeth and tapping the ground with a metal cane. The ragged children were racing after me and, unable to keep up, in their terrible hurry, breaking their pencil-thin legs. The old men and women were galloping all around me. I was pressing on full steam ahead! The dirty malnourished children, resembling poisonous mushrooms on thin stalks, were getting tangled up between my feet. It was difficult for me to run. I was constantly stumbling and, once, even came close to tumbling into the thick soup of the old men and women flailing on the ground. Hurdling over them, I decapitated several of the mushrooms and planted my foot firmly into the stomach of an emaciated old crone who, in reaction, emitted a resounding crunch and, in a resigned manner, pronounced: "It's the end of me." Without glancing back, I raced on. Presently, under my feet was a clean and even stone pavement. Occasional streetlights illuminated my way. I was quickly approaching a bathhouse. The friendly light of the bathhouse was already winking before me and the bathhouse's comforting yet suffocating steam was already crawling into my nostrils, ears, and mouth. Without undressing, I ran through the outer room, then past the row of spigots, showers, and tubs, and climbed up the shelf of benches. A steaming hot cloud surrounded me. I heard a muffled but insistent ringing. It seemed I was lying down.

. . . It was in that moment that my heart was seized by a mighty and powerful repose.

February 1, 1939

Fedya Davidovich

For a while now, Fedya had been eyeing the butter dish, and finally, seizing the moment when his wife bent down to trim a toenail, quickly in one motion drew the butter out of the dish with his finger and stuck it in his mouth. Closing the butter dish, Fedya accidentally tinkled the lid. The wife immediately straightened herself and, seeing the butter dish empty, pointed at it with the scissors and said in a stern voice:

There's no butter in the dish. Where is it?

Fedya, his eyes bulging with an expression of surprise, stretching his neck out, peered into the dish.

That's butter in your mouth, the wife said, pointing with the scissors at Fedya.

Fedya began wagging his head back and forth in denial.

Yes it is, said the wife. You are saying nothing and wagging your head because your mouth is stuffed with butter.

Fedya, his eyes bugged out even farther, started waving his arms in his wife's direction, as though saying: "What do you mean, what do you mean? Nothing of the sort!" But the wife said:

You're lying. Open your mouth.

Mm, said Fedya.

Open your mouth, the wife repeated.

Fedya, raising his hand up and spreading its fingers wide, began to moo, as though saying: "Ah, yes, I entirely forgot. I'll be right back," and got up, preparing to leave.

Stop, the wife yelled.

But Fedya quickened his pace and disappeared behind the door. The wife flung herself after him but stopped at the door because, being naked, she could not in such a state go out in the corridor, which was used by the other residents of the apartment.

He's gone, the wife said, sitting down on the sofa. What the!

Fedya, having walked the length of the corridor to a door on which hung a sign, "Entrance categorically forbidden," opened the door and entered the room.

The room Fedya entered was narrow and long, its only window covered with the pages of a newspaper. In the room, to the right, by the wall, stood a broken-down, dirty old couch, and by the window a table consisting of a board placed at one end on the night table, the other end resting on the back of a chair. On the wall to the left hung a double shelf, on which lay an indeterminate something. There was nothing else in the room, if one were not to count the man with the pale-green complexion lying on the couch, dressed in a long, torn brown morning coat and black flannel pants from which recently washed bare feet stuck out. The man was not at all sleeping, but rather intently watching the newly arrived.

Fedya bowed, shuffled his feet, and, having removed the butter from his mouth with his finger, showed it to the man lying on the couch.

One fifty, said the master of the room, without changing his position.

That's not enough, said Fedya.

It'll have to do, the master of the room said.

Alright then, Fedya said and, sliding the butter off his finger, smeared it onto the shelf.

Come for the money tomorrow morning, the master said.

Please, no! Fedya exclaimed. I need it now. It's only a ruble and a half . . .

Get lost, the master said tersely, and Fedya ran out of the room on tiptoe, carefully shutting the door behind him.

February 10, 1939

A Treatise, More or Less
in the Spirit of Emerson

I. On gifts

Imperfect gifts are the following kinds of gifts: we give a birthday celebrant a lid for an inkwell. And where's the inkwell itself? Or say we give an inkwell with a lid. And then where is the table on which the inkwell is supposed to stand? If the birthday celebrant already possesses a table, then the inkwell becomes a perfect gift. Therefore, if the birthday celebrant has an inkwell, then one may give him the lid alone, and then this would be a perfect gift. Decorations for the naked body, such as rings, bracelets, necklaces, etc. (assuming of course that the celebrant is not a cripple), would always be considered a perfect gift, or such gifts as a stick with a little wooden sphere attached at one end and a little wooden cube at the other. Such a stick may be held in one's hand or, if it is to be laid down, then it makes absolutely no difference where. Such a stick is of no use for any other purpose.

II. Of the proper surrounding of oneself with objects

Let us suppose that some entirely naked building superintendent decided to furnish and surround himself with objects. If he begins with a chair, then the chair will require a table, and the table a lamp, then a bed, a blanket, bedsheets, a dresser, underwear, a dress, a wardrobe, then a room where all of these may be placed, etc. Here, at each point in the system, may arise a little side system-branch: on the little round table one will want to place a cloth napkin, on the cloth napkin a vase, in the vase stick a flower. Such a system of surrounding oneself with objects, in which one so to speak overlaps with another object, is an incorrect system, because if the flower vase is missing flowers, then that vase becomes senseless, and if that vase is removed, then the little round table becomes senseless, though truth be told one might place on it a pitcher of water, but if one doesn't fill the pitcher with water, then the reasoning about the vase remains in force. The elimination of a single object. And if a naked building superintendent were to put on himself rings and bracelets and surround himself with spheres and plastic lizards, then the loss of a single or even of twenty-seven objects would have no bearing on the essence of the matter. Such a system of surrounding oneself with objects is a correct system.

III. On the correct destruction of objects surrounding oneself

A certain French writer of a commonly pedestrian bent, namely Alphonse Daudet, expressed an uninteresting thought that objects do not become attached to us but that we become attached to objects. Even the most unselfish person, having lost a watch, a coat, and a cupboard, will regret the loss. But even if we abolish our attachment to objects, then every person who had lost his bed and pillow, his floorboards, and even just some more or less comfortable rocks, having become acquainted with insomnia, will begin to regret the loss of these objects and of the comforts associated with them. Therefore, the destruction of objects collected according to an incorrect system of surrounding oneself with objects is—an incorrect system of the destruction of objects surrounding oneself. For, the destruction around oneself of always perfect gifts—wooden balls, plastic lizards, and so forth—will not present to a more or less unselfish person the least bit of regret. Destroying the objects surrounding oneself correctly, we lose appetite for every acquisition.

IV. On approaching immortality

It is characteristic of every person to strive toward enjoyment, which is always a kind of sexual fulfillment, either satisfaction or acquisition. But only that which does not lie on the path of enjoyment leads to immortality. All the systems leading toward immortality, in the final analysis, are reducible to a single rule: at all times do that which you do not want to do, because every person always wants to either eat, or to satisfy their sexual urges, or to acquire something, or all of the above, more or less, at once. Interestingly, immortality is always connected with death, and is represented by the various religious systems either as eternal enjoyment, or eternal suffering, or an eternal absence of both pleasure and suffering.

V. Of immortality

Righteous is he on whom God had bestowed life as a perfect gift.

February 14, 1939

NB: This is a stupid article.

The Old Woman [*Starukha*]

. . . And between them, the following conversation ensues.
—Hamsun

An old woman is standing in the yard, holding a wall clock in her arms. I walk past the crone, stop, and ask her: "What time is it?"

"Have a look," the old woman says.

I look closer and see that the clock is missing its hands.

"There are no hands," I say.

The old woman looks at the clock face and says:

"It is now a quarter to three."

"Is that so," I say and take my leave.

The old woman yells something after me, but I walk on without glancing back. I exit into the street and walk on the sunlit side. The spring sun feels simply wonderful. I am walking, squinting my eyes, and smoking a pipe. At the corner of the Garden Ring I cross paths with Sakerdon Mikhailovich walking towards me. We greet each other, stop, and chat for a long while. I become bored of standing in the street and invite Sakerdon Mikhailovich to accompany me inside a rathskeller. We drink vodka, chasing it down with hard-boiled eggs and salted fish, then say farewell, and I continue on my way alone.

Then I suddenly remember that I had forgotten to turn off the electric heater in my house. I turn around and walk back home. The day had begun so well and here already is the first misfortune. I should not have wandered away.

I come home, take off my coat, take my pocket watch out of the vest pocket, and hang it by its chain on a nail; then I lock the door with a key and lie down on the daybed. I will stay in bed and try to fall asleep.

I can hear the loathsome cries of boys coming from the street. I lie there, inventing ways to punish them. I like the idea of infecting them with tetanus best of these, so that they freeze in their tracks. And then the parents drag them to their homes. They lie in their little beds and can't even eat, because they can't open their mouths. They feed them artificially. The lockjaw passes in a week, but they are so weakened that for another full month they must stay between the sheets. Then they begin to gradually improve, but I make them relapse with another bout of tetanus, and they all perish.

I lie on the daybed with my eyes open and can't fall asleep. I remember the old woman with the wall clock whom I had seen in the yard today and a sense of contentment comes over me at her clock not having hands. Just the other day, in a consignment store, I saw the most abominable kitchen clock whose hands were made to look like a knife and a fork.

My Lord! I still haven't turned the electric heater off! I jump out of bed and turn it off, then again lie down on the daybed and try hard to fall asleep. I close my eyes. I don't feel like sleeping. The spring sun floods through the window and falls directly on me. I start feeling hot. I get up and sit down in the armchair by the window.

Now I feel sleepy, but I will not go to sleep. I will take out paper and quill and write. I sense in myself a terrible force. I had already planned it all out yesterday. It will be the tale of a miracle maker, who lives in our times and doesn't perform any miracles. He knows that he is a miracle maker and that he can perform any miracle, but he doesn't do it. He is evicted from his apartment, and he knows that with a wave of a handkerchief he could get his apartment back, but he doesn't do it, he meekly moves out of the apartment and lives in a barn outside of the city. He can transform this barn into a beautiful brick house, but he doesn't, and instead continues to live in the barn, and finally dies having never performed a single miracle.

I sit there and rub my hands together in glee. Sakerdon Mikhailovich will just die of envy. He thinks that I am no longer capable of producing a masterpiece. I must immediately get to work! Down with all sloth and slumber! I will now write for eighteen hours straight!

I am practically quivering with anticipation. I can't concentrate on the things at hand: I need to produce a quill and paper, and I am grabbing hold of various objects altogether different from the ones I intended to. I frantically pace the length of the room: from the window to the table, from the table to the wood-burning stove, from the stove back to the table, then to the couch and back again to the window. I am panting for air from the flame that is blazing in my breast. It is only five o'clock. Ahead of me is the entire day, the evening, and all of the night . . .

I stand in the middle of the room. What am I thinking of? It's already twenty minutes past five. I must write. I place the little writing table by the window and sit down at it. Before me is a pad of graphing paper and in my hand a quill.

My heart is still palpitating too much and my hand shakes. I wait until I calm down a bit. I put the quill down and fill my pipe. The sun is shining directly into my eyes; I squint and light the pipe.

A crow flies past the window. I look out the window onto the street and see how on the pavement walks a man with an artificial leg. He makes a racket with his leg and walking stick.

"OK," I say to myself, continuing to stare out the window.

The sun conceals itself behind the smokestack of the neighboring house. The shadow of the smokestack runs down the roof, flies across the street, and lies down on my face. I must make use of this shade and put down a few words about the miracle worker. I grab the quill and scribble:

"The miracle worker was a tall fellow."

I am not able to write anything more. I sit still until that time when I begin to feel hungry. Then I rise and walk over to the pantry, where I keep my provisions, and run my hand along all the surfaces but find nothing in it. A cube of sugar and that's about it.

Somebody's knocking at the door.

"Who's there?"

Nobody answers me. I open the door and see before me the old crone who had stood in the morning with a wall clock in the yard. I am very surprised and cannot get a word out.

"Well, I've come," the old woman says and enters my room.

I stand by the door, not knowing what to do: do I chase the old woman out or the opposite, invite her in to sit down? But the old crone walks towards the window armchair on her own accord and plants herself in it.

"Close the door and put the lock on," the old woman says.

I close the door and lock it.

"Get on your knees," the old woman says.

And I get down on my knees.

But then I begin to understand how preposterous my situation is. Why am I standing on my knees before some old crone? And how did this old crone make her way into my room and is now sitting in my favorite armchair? Why did I not chase the old woman out?

"Now hear this," I say. "Who gave you the right to issue orders in my place, and even boss me around? I have no desire to be standing on my knees."

"You don't have to," the old woman says. "Now you must lie down on your stomach and plaster your face to the floor."

I immediately execute her command.

I see in front of my nose precisely drawn squares. The pain in my shoulder and right hip force me to change my position. I lie completely prone and can now raise myself to my knees only with great difficulty. The blood has pooled in all my extremities and they bend very poorly. I gaze backwards and see myself in my own room, standing on my knees in the middle of the floor. My awareness and memory slowly return to me. I look around the room once again and see that apparently someone is seated in the armchair by the window. The room is barely lit because the white nights, it seems, are just beginning. I look more closely. Good Lord! Could it be that the old crone is still sitting in my chair? I stretch my neck out to see better. Yes, of course, the old woman is sitting there with her head drooping down on her chest. She must've fallen asleep.

I get up and, limping a bit, walk over to her. The old woman's head is lowered to her chest, her arms are hanging down the side of the armchair. I want to grab this old crone and shove her out the door.

"Listen to me," I say. "You are in my room. I have to work. I ask you to please leave."

The old woman doesn't budge. I bend over and look at the old woman's face. Her mouth is ajar and poking out of her mouth are her dentures that have become detached. Suddenly, everything becomes perfectly clear to me: the crone has died.

I am overcome by a terrible sense of annoyance. Why did she have to die in my room? I can't stand stiffs. And now there's the hassle of dealing with this roadkill, go have a talk with the porter, the super, explain it to them, how this old woman ended up in my place. I look at the crone with loathing. Maybe perhaps she isn't dead after all? I feel her forehead. The forehead is cold. The arm also. What am I to do?

I light my pipe and sit down on the daybed. A blind rage wells up in me.

"That bitch!" I say out loud.

The dead woman is sitting in my armchair like a sack of potatoes. Her teeth are protruding out of her mouth. She resembles a dead horse.

"What a revolting sight," I say, but can't force myself to cover the old woman with a newspaper, because you never know what might happen under the newspaper.

I can hear something moving on the other side of the wall: it's my neighbor, the train mechanic. It couldn't get much worse, if he were to get a whiff of what was going on, that sitting in my room was a dead old crone! I perk up my ears to hear my neighbor's steps. Why is he dawdling? It's already half past five! He should have been long gone by now. My God! He's making tea. Beyond the wall I hear the whistle of a teakettle. Ah, let him go off already, the damn mechanic!

I climb with my feet up on the daybed and lie there. Eight minutes pass by, but the neighbor has yet to have his tea, and the kettle's still hissing. I close my eyes and doze off.

I dream that my neighbor has gone out and that I go out in the stairwell along with him and slam the door with the French lock behind me. I didn't take a key and can't get back inside the apartment. I will have to ring their bells and wake the rest of my neighbors, and this is really too much. I stand on the landing in the stairwell and think about what I should do, and suddenly I see that I'm missing my hands. I bend my head to get a closer look, to check if I do have hands, and see that on one side, instead of a hand, I have a table knife sticking out, and on the other side, a fork.

"Look at this," I say to Sakerdon Mikhailovich, who for some reason is sitting right there on a folding chair. "Do you see this," I tell him, "the kind of hands I have?"

And Sakerdon Mikhailovich sits there silently and I see that it's not the real Sakerdon Mikhailovich but a clay one.

At this point I awake and immediately understand that I am lying in my room on the daybed, and by the window, in the armchair, sits a dead old woman.

I quickly turn my head toward her. And the old woman's gone. I look at the empty armchair and am filled with wild joy. That means it was all a dream. Only where did it begin? Did the old crone enter my room yesterday? Perhaps that too was a dream? I returned home yesterday because I forgot to turn off the electric heater. But maybe that too was a dream? In any case, how wonderful that there is no dead old crone in my room, and that means that I don't have to see the super and deal with the stiff.

However, how long did I sleep? I look at the pocket watch on the wall: half past nine, must be in the morning.

"Good Lord! The things one sees in dreams!"

I lower my feet from the daybed, and am about to get up when I see the dead old woman lying on the floor by the table, beside the armchair. She is lying face up, and the dentures, having escaped her mouth, are hanging on by a tooth onto one of the old crone's nostrils. Her hands have become tangled underneath her and are invisible, and from under her hiked-up skirt stick out bony feet clad in dirty white woolen socks.

"You bitch!" I scream and, running over to her, kick her in the chin with my boot.

The dentures come flying out into the corner. I want to kick the old woman once more but am afraid that if I leave any marks on her body, they might just decide later that I killed her. Some twenty minutes pass in this manner. Now it becomes perfectly clear to me that they would, after all, turn the case into a criminal investigation anyway, and the dumb detectives will accuse me of murder.

I step away from the old crone, sit down on the daybed, and light my pipe. Looks like it's going to be no laughing matter, and here I am kicking her with my boots.

I walk over to the old woman again, bend over her, and begin examining her face. On her chin is a small dark spot. Don't think they'll try to pin that on me. It could have been anything. The crone could have knocked her chin on something while she was alive. I calm down a bit and begin to pace the room, smoking my pipe and pondering my predicament.

I pace around the room and begin to feel hunger, progressively more intense. I even begin to shiver from hunger. I rummage through the pantry where my provisions are kept one more time but find nothing besides the cube of sugar.

I take out my wallet and count my money. Eleven rubles. This means I can buy myself some ham and bread, and still have some left over for tobacco.

I fix my tie that had come askew during the night, take my watch, put on my coat, carefully lock the door to my apartment, put the key in my pocket, and walk out into the street. Before anything else, I must get something to eat, then my thoughts will become clearer and that way I will be able to do something about that piece of carrion.

On my way to the store, yet another thought crosses my mind: maybe I should go over to Sakerdon Mikhailovich's and tell him everything, and perhaps, together we will think of something to do. But I immediately reject this idea, because some things are best done alone, without any witnesses.

At the store, they don't have any ham cold cuts, so I buy myself a half a kilo of wursts. There is also no tobacco. From the delicatessen I head to the bakery.

The bakery is crowded and there is a long line at the checkout counter. My spirits immediately flag but I still get in line. The line moves very slowly, and then stops entirely, because some sort of a scandal has erupted at the cash register.

I act as though nothing is happening, and stare at the back of the young girl who is standing in front of me. The young ladyship is, apparently, very curious: she keeps stretching her neck out, first to the right, then to the left, constantly getting on her tippy-toes so as to better see what is going on at the cash register. Finally, she turns back to face me and says:

"You don't happen to know what's going on over there?"

"Forgive me, I do not," I say as dryly as possible.

Her ladyship twists and turns in every direction and finally again addresses herself to me:

"You wouldn't be willing to go and find out what's happening over there?"

"Forgive me, but it doesn't interest me in the least," I say even more dryly than before.

"What do you mean it doesn't interest you?" her ladyship exclaims. "You're being held back in line because of it as well!"

I say nothing in response and only bow my head slightly. Her ladyship looks at me intently.

"Of course, it's not a manly affair, to stand in lines for bread," she says. "I feel pity for you, that you should have to stand here. You must be a bachelor?"

"Yes, a bachelor," I say, somewhat distracted from my line of thought, but out of inertia, continue answering rather dryly while simultaneously bowing slightly.

Her ladyship looks me over one more time from head to foot and suddenly, touching her fingers to my sleeve, says:

"Let me buy you what you need and you can go wait for me in the street."

I lose my poise entirely.

"I am grateful to you," I say. "That is very kind of you, but, really, I can manage for myself."

"No, no," her ladyship says. "Step out into the street. What was it you were getting for yourself?"

"You see," I say, "I was planning to buy a half kilo of black bread, but only the unsliced kind, the one that's cheaper. I like it more."

"Well, that's well and good," her ladyship says. "Now you're free to go. I'll buy it, and you can pay me back later, outside."

And she even gives me a slight push on the elbow.

I go outside the bakery and stand right by the door. The spring sun is shining directly in my face. I light my pipe. What a kind young lady. That's so rare these days. I stand there, squinting from the sun, smoke my pipe, and think about the kind young lady. She has pretty little light hazel eyes. It's just wonderful how pretty she is!

"You smoke a pipe?" I hear a voice beside me. The kind young lady is handing me my bread.

"Oh. I am endlessly grateful to you," I say, taking the bread.

"So you smoke a pipe! I like that very much," the kind young lady says.

And between us transpires the following conversation.

SHE: So, it appears that you go to buy bread for yourself.

I: And not just bread. I buy everything for myself.

SHE: And where do you eat it?

I: I usually make dinner for myself. And occasionally I go out to eat at a bar.

SHE: So you like beer?

I: No, I prefer vodka.

SHE: I like vodka too!

I: You like vodka? Well, that's wonderful! I would love to have a drink together sometime.

SHE: And I too, would like to have some vodka together.

I: Forgive me, but may I ask you just one thing?

SHE (blushing considerably): Of course, ask away.

I: OK, I will go ahead then. Do you believe in God?

SHE (surprised): In God? Yes, of course.

I: And what would you say if we were to buy some vodka now and go over to my place? I live nearby.

SHE (excitedly): Well, yes! I agree!

I: Let us go then.

We go into a store, and I buy a half a liter of vodka. It's the last of my money, only some coins left. We continue talking about all sorts of things and I suddenly remember that on the floor, in my room, lies the body of an old woman.

I look over at my new lady acquaintance: she's standing by the counter and examining jars of preserves. I silently move toward the door and leave the store. Just then, opposite the store, a streetcar comes to a stop. I jump on, without even looking at the streetcar number. I get out at Mikhailovsky Street and walk to Sakerdon Mikhailovich's. In my hands are a bottle of vodka, wursts, and bread.

Sakerdon Mikhailovich answers the door himself. He is wearing a robe, thrown over his naked body, in Russian leather boots with their shins sliced off, and a hat with fur earflaps, but the flaps are raised and tied at the top of his head in a bowtie.

"Very happy to see you," says Sakerdon Mikhailovich, seeing that it's me.

"I'm not taking you away from your work?" I ask.

"No, not at all," says Sakerdon Mikhailovich. "I wasn't doing anything, just sitting on the floor."

"As you see," I say to Sakerdon Mikhailovich, "I have come to you with some vodka and snacks. If you have nothing against it, let's have a drink together."

"Very well," says Sakerdon Mikhailovich, "please come in."

We go through into his room. I unstopper the bottle of vodka, and Sakerdon Mikhailovich places on the table two shot glasses and a plate of boiled meat.

"I brought some wursts," I say. "So, how shall we have them, uncooked, or do we boil them?"

"We will put them on to boil," says Sakerdon Mikhailovich, "while we ourselves will be drinking vodka between bites of boiled meat. I took it out of the soup, excellent boiled meat!"

Sakerdon Mikhailovich puts a pot on the kerosene camper stove, and we sit down to drink vodka.

"Vodka's good for you," says Sakerdon Mikhailovich, filling our shot glasses. "Metchnikoff wrote that vodka is better for you than bread, that bread is just hay, which rots in our stomachs."

"To your health!" I say, clinking glasses with Sakerdon Mikhailovich. We gulp the vodka and wash it down with some cold meat.

"Delicious," says Sakerdon Mikhailovich.

But that very moment, something in the room cracks.

"What's that?" I ask.

We sit quietly trying to make out the sound. Suddenly, there is a second crack. Sakerdon Mikhailovich jumps out of his chair and, having run over to the window, tears the curtain down.

"What are you doing?" I scream.

But Sakerdon Mikhailovich, without answering me, bolts for the camper stove, grabs the pot with the curtain, and places it down on the floor.

"Damn it!" says Sakerdon Mikhailovich. "I forgot to fill the pot with water. The little pot is enamel, and now the enamel has popped."

"Now I understand," I say, nodding my head.

We sit down again at the table.

"Screw it!" says Sakerdon Mikhailovich, "we'll eat the wursts raw."

"I am so very hungry," say I.

"Eat, eat," says Sakerdon Mikhailovich, moving the sausages towards me.

"The last time I ate was yesterday, with you, in the pub, and I haven't had a bite since," I say.

"Yes, yes, yes," says Sakerdon Mikhailovich.

"I was writing the whole time."

"That's damn good!" Sakerdon Mikhailovich yells out melodramatically. "It's a privilege to be in the presence of a genius."

"You don't say!" say I.

"I s'ppose you really piled it on?" Sakerdon Mikhailovich asks.

"Yep," say I. "Used up whole reams and reams of paper."

"A toast to the genius of our times," says Sakerdon Mikhailovich, raising his shot glass.

We down a shot. Sakerdon Mikhailovich eats the boiled meat and I eat the wursts. Having eaten four of the sausages, I light my pipe and say:

"You know, I came to you to escape persecution."

"Who was it that was after you?" asks Sakerdon Mikhailovich.

"A lady," say I.

But because Sakerdon Mikhailovich doesn't follow up with a question and instead in silence pours two more shots, I continue:

"I met her at the bakery and immediately fell in love with her."

"Is she pretty?" asks Sakerdon Mikhailovich.

"Yes," I say, "just my type."

We have another shot, and I continue:

"She agreed to come over to my place to drink vodka. We went into a store, but I had no choice but to quietly vamoose from the premises."

"You ran out of money?" asks Sakerdon Mikhailovich.

"No, the money was just enough, but I remembered that I couldn't let her into my room."

"Ah, so there was another lady in your room?" Sakerdon Mikhailovich asks.

"Yes, if you'd like to put it that way, in my room is another lady," I say, smiling. "And now I can't allow anyone into it."

"Get married. You'll be able to invite me over for dinner," says Sakerdon Mikhailovich.

"No way," I say, snorting with laughter. "I'm never marrying this one."

"Then marry the other, the one from the bakery," says Sakerdon Mikhailovich.

"Why are you always trying to get me married off?" say I.

"And why not?" says Sakerdon Mikhailovich, filling our shot glasses. "To your future conquests!"

We drink. It seems the effects of the vodka on us have become noticeable. Sakerdon Mikhailovich takes off his fur hat with the ear-flaps and flings it on his bed. I get up and stroll across the room, already feeling in my head a certain spinning sensation.

"And what is your attitude toward stiffs?" I ask Sakerdon Mikhailovich.

"Negative in the extreme," says Sakerdon Mikhailovich. "I'm afraid of them."

"Yes, I too can't stand them," say I. "Should I happen to cross paths with a stiff, and if it's not my relative, I expect I would give him a good stiff kick."

"There's no need to be kicking dead folk," says Sakerdon Mikhailovich.

"But I would too, kick them, right in the mug, with my boot. I simply can't stand stiffs, or children."

"Yes, children are vile creatures," Sakerdon Mikhailovich agrees.

"And which do you think are worse, stiffs or children?" I ask.

"Children probably are worse; they are more often in the way. Stiffs, after all, do not intrude themselves into our lives," says Sakerdon Mikhailovich.

"Intrude and how!" I scream and immediately shut up.

Sakerdon Mikhailovich examines me, slowly and attentively.

"Would you like some more vodka?" he asks.

"No," say I, but coming to my senses add: "No thank you. No more for me."

I walk back over to the table and again sit down. We sit this way for some time in silence.

"I would like to ask you something," I finally say. "Do you believe in God?"

A deep horizontal crease flashes across Sakerdon Mikhailovich's forehead, and he says:

"There is such a thing as a rude deed. It is bad manners, for example, to ask to borrow fifty rubles from a man when you've just seen him put two hundred rubles in his pocket. It's his business, whether to give you the money or to refuse it, and the most pleasant way to say no is to lie about it and say you haven't got any money. But you've just seen that the man has money and thereby deprived him of the possibility of denying you in the simplest, most congenial way. You've stripped him of his freedom to choose, and that is despicable. This is a brazen and indecent act. And to ask a man whether he believes in God, that is likewise a tactless and boorish act."

"Well," I say. "But these two have nothing in common."

"And I am not comparing the two," says Sakerdon Mikhailovich.

"Point well taken," I say. "Let us drop it then. Only please, do forgive me for asking such a rude, indelicate question."

"I didn't mean it that way," says Sakerdon Mikhailovich. "After all, I had simply refused to answer you."

"I would have also refused to answer it," say I, "but only for a different reason."

"And what reason is that?" Sakerdon Mikhailovich asks tepidly.

"You see," I say, "it seems to me that there are no believers or disbelievers. There are only those who wish to believe and those who wish not to believe."

"So you mean that those who wish not to believe already believe in something?" says Sakerdon Mikhailovich. "And those who wish to believe already, a priori, do not believe in anything?"

"It may be so," say I. "I do not know."

"But believe or disbelieve in what? In God?" asks Sakerdon Mikhailovich.

"No," I say. "In immortality."

"Then why did you ask me if I believe in God or not?"

"Well, simply because asking 'Do you or do you not believe in immortality?' sounds somehow foolish," I say to Sakerdon Mikhailovich and get up from the table.

"Are you going then?" Sakerdon Mikhailovich asks me.

"Yes," I say. "It's time for me to go."

"And what about the vodka?" says Sakerdon Mikhailovich. "There's just a shot left for each of us."

"Alright, let's finish it," say I.

We down the rest of the vodka and chase it with the remnants of the boiled meat.

"And now I must go," I say.

"Till our next meeting," says Sakerdon Mikhailovich, seeing me off through the kitchen to the stairwell. "Thank you for the treat."

"Thank you," I say. "Good-bye."

And I leave.

Left alone, Sakerdon Mikhailovich clears the table, tosses the empty bottle on top of the wardrobe, puts the fur hat with the ear-flaps back on his head, and sits down on the floor beneath the window. He places his hands behind his back, so that they are invisible. His naked, bony legs, shod in Russian boots, their shins removed, are sticking out from under his hiked-up robe.

I walk along Nevsky Prospect, deeply immersed in my own thoughts. I must go see the super immediately and tell him everything. And, after I've dealt with the crone, I'll stand outside the bakery for days, until I see that kind young woman again. I still owe her forty-eight kopeks for the bread. I have a wonderful pretext for trying to find her. The vodka I have drunk is still exerting its attraction, and it seems that everything is coming together rather nicely, even swimmingly.

On the Fontaka, I stroll over to the kiosk and, with the remaining change, buy myself a large mug of bread kvass. The kvass is stale and sour, and I walk on with a nasty taste in my mouth.

At the corner of Liteiny Prospect, some staggering drunk shoves me. I'm glad I don't own a gun: I would have shot him right there and then.

I walk the rest of the way home with my face contorted by rage. In any case, everyone walking toward me turns around to look at me as I pass them by.

I walk into the apartment building office. A squat, lopsided, dirty young woman with a turned-up nose and hair devoid of all pigment is sitting on top of the table, looking into her handheld mirror, and smearing her mouth with lipstick.

"Where's the super?" I ask.

The girl remains silent, continuing to apply her lipstick.

"Where's the super?" I repeat brusquely.

"He'll be in tomorrow, not today," the dirty, pig-nosed, misshapen, flaxen-haired girl replies.

I go out into the street. Walking on the opposite side is a disabled man with an artificial leg who is making a loud racket with his leg and walking stick. Six boys are running after him, making fun of the way he walks.

I turn into the lobby of my building and start climbing the stairs. On the second floor, I stop; a disturbing thought has come into my head: the old crone's probably begun decomposing by now. I hadn't closed the windows, and they say that corpses start decomposing faster if the windows are left open. What a nuisance! And that nincompoop of a super won't be in until tomorrow! I stand there in my hesitation for several minutes and then resume climbing the stairs.

I pause once again at the door of my apartment. Perhaps I better walk over to the bakery instead and wait there for that kind young lady? I would beg her to let me stay with her for two or three nights. But then I remember that she has already bought bread, which means that she won't be visiting the bakery again today. And even if she does, nothing will come of it anyway.

I unlock the door and enter the hallway. At the end of the corridor, a light shines, and Mariya Vasilievna, who is holding in her hand some sort of rag, is scrubbing it with another rag. Noticing me, Mariya Vasilievna shouts:

"Shom ol' man wazh ashking for you!"

"What old man?" I say.

"I can't shay," Mariya Vasilievna answers.

"When was this?" I ask.

"Alsho can't shay," Mariya Vasilievna says.

"Was it you who spoke with him?" I ask Mariya Vasilievna.

"T'wazh me," Mariya Vasilievna answers.

"Then how can you possibly not know what time it was?" I say.

"Shom two ourzh ago," says Mariya Vasilievna.

"And what did this old man look like?" I ask.

"Alsho can't shay," Mariya Vasilievna says and heads toward the kitchen.

I walk toward my room. What if, I think to myself, the old woman has vanished? I will enter the room, and the crone will be gone. Lordy lord! Is there really no such thing as a miracle in our day and age?

I unlock my room and begin to swing the door slowly open.

Perhaps it only seems so to me, but the sickly sweet odor of the early stages of decomposition wafts up into my face. I peek inside the partly ajar door and, for a split second, freeze in my tracks. The old woman is slowly crawling toward me on all fours.

I slam the door shut with a holler, turn the key, and jump back against the opposite wall.

Mariya Vasilievna appears in the hallway once again.

"You wanted shomething?" she asks.

I am trembling so badly that I can't get a word out and only wag my head to indicate "No." Mariya Vasilievna approaches closer.

"Were you shpeaking with shomeone?" she says.

I once again shake my head in denial.

"Got a shcrew loosh," Mariya Vasilievna says and once again heads for the kitchen, glancing over her shoulder at me several times on her way back.

"I mustn't stand around like this. I mustn't stand around like this," I keep repeating over and over in my mind. This unbidden phrase has composed itself somewhere deep in my bowels, and I keep muttering it again and again until it floats up into my consciousness.

"Yes indeed, I mustn't stand around like this," I say to myself, but continue standing there, paralyzed. Something horrifying has happened, but I am faced with the prospect of having to do something perhaps much worse than what has already occurred. My thoughts are swirling in eddies, and all I can make out are the eyes of the dead old crone slowly crawling towards me on all fours.

To burst into the room and smash the old crone's skull into smithereens. That's what I must do! I even look around me and am happy to find a croquet mallet, which for no discernible reason has been standing around for many years now in the corner of the corridor. All I have to do is seize the mallet, burst into the room, and whack!

I am still shaking. I stand there with my shoulders raised and head retracted as though to ward off the inner cold. My thoughts are racing, becoming jumbled, returning to their point of departure and then again beginning to gallop, spreading over new domains, but I keep perfectly still, trying to listen in on my own thoughts, as though I am standing outside of them and am not their captain.

"Stiffs are a quirky lot," my own thoughts are explaining to me. "'Deceased' is a misnomer for them; 'dis-eased' is more like it. You always have to keep an eye out for them. You can ask any morgue attendant. Why do you think they have them posted there? For one reason only: to make sure the cadavers don't crawl away. There have been many curious incidents in this respect. One stiff, while the guard was taking a bath on orders from the management, crawled out of the morgue and, finding his way into the disinfection chamber, ate a pile of bedsheets there. The orderlies who worked there gave this stiff a good beating, but they still had to make up for the spoiled sheets out of their own pockets. And another cadaver crawled into the maternity ward and scared the expectant mothers so badly that one of them immediately dropped a preemie, a miscarriage, and the stiff pounced on the discarded fetus and started devouring it, chomping loudly. And when one brave nurse clobbered the stiff over his back with a footstool, he managed to snag this nurse's foot in his choppers, and she came down with toxic syndrome and shortly thereafter perished. Yes, stiffs are indeed a questionable lot, and one must always stay vigilant around them."

"Enough!" I address my own thoughts. "You're talking nonsense. Stiffs are immobile."

"Alright, then," my own thoughts are saying to me, "why don't you just go ahead and enter your room where, as you say, the immobile stiff is reposing."

A sudden obstinacy wells up in me.

"And I will, too!" I say decisively to my own thoughts.

"Just you try!" my own thoughts say to me.

This mocking finally succeeds in infuriating and driving me over the edge. I grab the croquet mallet and fling myself at the door.

"Wait!" my own thoughts scream in my wake. But I have already turned the key and thrown the door open.

The old woman is lying prone near the threshold, her face peeled to the floor.

I stand above her with the croquet mallet raised at the ready. The old woman lies still.

The shivering has left me, and my thoughts are now flowing, lucidly and precisely. I am once again their master.

"First of all, you must close the door!" I command myself.

I remove the key from the outside of the door and insert it on the inside. I perform this with my left hand, continuing to hold the croquet mallet in my right, while not taking my eyes off the old woman for a split second. I lock the door with the key and, having carefully stepped over the old woman, stride out into the middle of the room.

"And now we will settle our accounts with you," I say.

I have hatched a plan, the sort that killers in crime fiction novels and police blotter columns commonly resort to; I will simply stuff the old woman in a suitcase, take it outside the city, and dump her into a swamp. I even know one such place.

And the suitcase is standing under my couch. I drag it out and open the lid. It contains the following assortment of things: several books, an old fedora, and ragged bedsheets and undergarments. I take all of these out and lay them on the daybed.

At that moment, the outer door is slammed shut, and it seems to me that the old woman shudders.

I immediately spring up and grab the croquet mallet.

The old woman is lying very still. I hold my breath and listen carefully. It is the motorman, home from work: I can hear him pacing around in his room. Now he is walking to the kitchen along the corridor. If Mariya Vasilievna recounts to him my bout of insanity it won't end well. What the devil! I will also have to take a walk over to the kitchen and calm them down by making an appearance.

I again step over the old woman, place the croquet mallet close by the door, so that when I return I can, without entering the room, have it handy. I can hear voices issuing from the kitchen, but I can't make out any of the words. I close the door behind me and warily start toward the kitchen: I want to find out what it is that Mariya Vasilievna and the motorman are discussing. I walk the corridor briskly, slowing down near the kitchen, where I hear footsteps. The motorman is speaking; it seems he is describing something that has happened to him at work.

I enter. The motorman is standing with a towel in his hands and speaking, and Mariya Vasilievna is sitting on a footstool and listening. Seeing me enter, the motorman waves his hand.

"Good day, good day, Matvei Philipovich," I say to him, and walk past them to the bathroom. So far so good. Mariya Vasilievna has gotten accustomed to my eccentricities and may have already forgotten the last occasion.

Suddenly it dawns on me: I haven't locked the door! What if the old crone were to crawl out of the room?

I lunge backward, but catch myself in time and, taking care not to alarm the neighbors, stroll through the kitchen at a calm and measured pace.

Mariya Vasilievna is drumming the kitchen table with her fingers and saying to the motorman:

"That's shvel! Wow, that'sh wonderful! I'd be whishtling too!"

With my heart in my throat, I go out into the corridor and at once almost break into a dash back to my room.

On the outside, everything is peaceful. I approach the door and, having pushed it ajar, peek inside the room. The old woman is lying peacefully as before, her face pinned to the floor. The croquet mallet is standing by the door where I had left it. I pick it up, enter the room, and lock the door behind myself. Yes, the room definitely stinks of putrefying flesh. I step over the old woman, walk over to the window, and sit down in the armchair. I only hope that I won't start to retch from the as yet faint but still unbearable odor. I light my pipe. I am getting nauseous, and my stomach has begun to ache.

What am I sitting here for? I must act immediately, before this old woman really begins to stink this place up. But, just in case, I will need to be careful when I stuff her inside the suitcase, because that's exactly when she's likely to take a chunk out of my finger. And then there's nothing to do but die of toxic shock—yes, thank you very much!

"Ah, so!" I exclaim suddenly. "I'm curious what exactly you plan to bite me with? Your choppers are way over yonder!"

I bend over in my armchair and look down in the corner on the other side of the room where, according to my calculations, the old woman's dentures must have landed. But her false teeth aren't there.

I start thinking that perhaps, when the dead crone was crawling around my room, she was searching for her teeth. Perhaps she even found them and inserted them back in her mouth.

I pick up the croquet mallet and shuffle it around, deep in the corner. No use, the dentures have vanished. I then remove a thick flannel sheet out of the dresser and bring it over to the old woman. I clutch the croquet mallet in my right hand, holding the flannel bedsheet in my left.

The sight of the old woman produces in me a sense of squeamish dread and revulsion. I use the tip of the mallet to hook the old woman's head and raise it up off the floor: her mouth hangs open, her eyes rolled upwards, and, where I had kicked her, a large dark stain has begun to spread across her entire chin. I peek inside the old woman's mouth. No, she has not found her false teeth. I let go of the head and it drops to the floor with a thud.

I then proceed to spread the flannel sheet on the floor and pull it just under the old woman. Then, with the mallet and the side of my foot, I turn the old woman over, across her left side and onto her back. She is now lying on top of the bedsheet. The old woman's legs are bent at the knees, and her fists are clenched shut at her shoulders. It seems that the crone, lying on her back like a cat, is about to defend herself from a bird of prey that is about to pounce on her. Get this carrion out of here quick!

I roll the old woman inside the thick sheet and lift her up in my arms. She turns out to be lighter than I had imagined. I lower her into the suitcase and attempt to seal the lid shut. I am expecting all sorts of difficulties in this, but the lid closes with relative ease. I snap the metal latches of the suitcase shut and, straightening out my back, rise to my full height.

The suitcase is standing before me, by the looks of it quite legitimate, as though laden with bedding and books. Grasping it by the handle, I attempt to lift it. Yes, it is, of course, heavy, but moderately so; I will have no trouble getting it to the tram stop.

I look at the clock: it is twenty minutes past five. That's good. I sit back down in my armchair, to rest up a bit and smoke my pipe.

My guess is that the spoiled sausages I ate earlier have disagreed with me, because my upset stomach is getting worse by the minute. Or is it because I ate them raw? Who knows, perhaps the pains in my stomach are purely a nervous reaction.

I am sitting here and smoking. Minute after minute flies by.

The spring sun floods in through the window, and I am squinting from its bright rays. There it goes again behind the smokestack of the building on the opposite side of the street, and the shadow of the smokestack glides across the roof, flies across the street, and lands on my face. I recall how, at this very same time of day, yesterday, I was sitting here, writing a story. Here it is: the graphing paper, and on it, an inscription in microscopic handwriting. "The miracle worker was a tall fellow."

I look out of the window. Passing by in the street, I see the disabled man with the artificial leg, his leg and cane banging loudly. Two laborers and the old woman with them are howling at the disabled man's peculiar gait, holding their sides, as if splitting from laughter.

I get up. It's time to go! Time for me to get on the road. It's time to take the old woman to the swamp! But before I go, I must still ask the motorman to borrow some money.

I go out into the corridor and walk over to the door of his room.

"Matvei Philipovich, are you in?" I ask.

"Home," the motorman answers.

"Then, please forgive me, Matvei Philipovich, but you wouldn't happen to have been paid? I'm not getting mine till the day after tomorrow. You wouldn't be so kind as to let me borrow thirty rubles?"

"Can do," the motorman says. And I hear how he is jangling his keys, opening some sort of lockbox. Then he opens the door and stretches out his hand with a crisp new red thirty-ruble bill.

"Thank you kindly, Matvei Philipovich," I say.

"Don't mention it, don't mention it," says the motorman.

I shove the money in my pocket and return to my room. The suitcase is still standing undisturbed in its previous place.

"And now we'll be off without any further delays," I say to myself.

I pick up the suitcase and exit the room.

Mariya Vasilievna sees me with the suitcase and shouts out:

"Where you off to?"

"To my auntie's," I say.

"Coming back shoon?" Mariya Vasilievna asks.

"Yes," I say. "I just need to take some linens over to my auntie's. I might even be back later tonight."

I go out into the street. I make it to the streetcar stop without anything out of the ordinary happening, taking turns carrying the suitcase first in the right, then in the left hand.

I climb onto the tram from the front landing of the second car and start waving to the woman conductor for her to come over and collect my ticket fare and the surcharge for the luggage. I do not want to pass my only thirty-ruble note the length of the entire car and don't dare leave the suitcase unattended and walk over to the conductor lady myself. The conductor lady walks back to my landing and declares that she doesn't have change to break my bill. I have to climb off at the very first stop.

I stand there fuming and wait for the next tram. My stomach is aching and my legs are trembling noticeably.

And suddenly I catch sight of my sweet young lady: she is crossing the street and not looking in my direction.

I grab the suitcase and run after her. I don't know her name and so am unable to call out to her. The suitcase is making it awfully difficult: I keep it in front of me, carrying it with both of my hands and shoving it with my knees and stomach. The kind young lady is walking quite briskly, and I know I won't be able to catch up to her. By now, I am drenched in sweat and dropping from exhaustion. The sweet young lady turns the corner down an alleyway and, by the time I have reached the corner, is nowhere to be seen.

Damn old crone! I hiss out, tossing the suitcase on the ground.

The sleeves of my coat are soaked through with sweat and sticking to my hands. Two boys stop in front of me and begin examining me. I put on a calm demeanor and am staring intently over at the nearest passageway, pretending I am waiting for someone. The boys are whispering to each other and pointing at me with their fingers. I am suffocating with the most seething animosity. If only I could infect these two with lockjaw!

And so, because of these wretched urchins, I rise, pick up the suitcase, drag it over to the passageway, and peek inside it. I mime an expression of surprise, pull out my pocket watch, and shrug my shoulders. The boys are observing me from a distance. I shrug my shoulders once again and crane my neck to look down the alley.

"Strange," I say out loud, pick up the suitcase, and drag it once more back to the streetcar stop.

I arrive at the train station at five to seven. I buy a round-trip ticket to Lisy Nos and board the train.

In the car besides me are two others; one, it seems, is a laborer: he is tired and sleeps, having pulled his cap over his eyes. The other, still a young man, is dressed like a provincial fop: peeking out from under his suit jacket is a collarless homespun pink shirt, and protruding from under his cap is a coiffed, wavy cowlick. He is smoking a hand-rolled cigarette, stuck into a bright green plastic holder.

I place the suitcase down between the benches and sit down. My belly is hurting so badly that I have to clench my fists to keep from groaning out loud from the pain.

Along the platform, two policemen are leading away some sort of upstanding citizen off to a holding cell. He is walking with his hands folded behind his back, his head crestfallen.

The train jolts and starts moving. I look down at my watch: it is ten past seven.

Oh, with what joy I will dump this old crone into the bog! I only regret that I didn't think to bring the stick along; she'll probably require a good nudge.

The dandy in the pink homespun shirt is looking me over impudently. I turn my back to him and look out the window.

My stomach is churning with terrible cramps, and I clench my teeth, ball up my fists, and tense my legs.

We pass Lansky Station and New Village. Over there, you can see the gilded top of the Buddhist pagoda flashing by, and over there, a glimmer of the sea.

That very second I jump up and, forgetting everything, run to the toilet with short, stuttering, constrained steps. My consciousness is contorted by a sickening wave of rocking and spinning. . . .

The train slows down. We're approaching Lakhta. I am sitting absolutely still, afraid to let out a peep, so that they don't chase me out of the toilet while the train is stopped.

Let the train start already! Come on, let's go!

The train moves, and I close my eyes in delight. Oh, these minutes can be so sweet at times, like the moments we are making love! All my senses tense up, concentrated in this moment, but I know that what follows will be a terrible letdown.

The train once again comes to a stop. This must be Olgino. Which means the same torture all over again!

But now, these are false urges. A cold sweat begins to bead my forehead, and a slight chill flutters around my heart. I rise and for some time stand with my forehead pressed to the wall. The train is moving, and its rocking motion feels quite soothing to me.

I gather my remaining strength and, stumbling, exit the restroom.

The train car is empty. The working man and the dandy in the pink handspun shirt, it appears, must have gotten off at Lakhta or Olgino. I walk slowly over to my window.

And suddenly I stop and stare ahead of myself stupefied. The suitcase is not where I had left it. I must have confused the windows. I run over to the next window seat. No suitcase there either. I run back and forth, racing the length of the car, checking both sides of the aisle, peeking under the seats, but the suitcase is nowhere to be found.

Can there be any doubt? Of course, the suitcase was stolen while I was on the toilet. This could have been foreseen!

I sit on the bench with my eyes bulging and, for some reason, am reminded of how, at Sakerdon Mikhailovich's, the enamel had come off with a pop from the little scalding hot cooking pot.

"So what have we got here?" I ask myself.

Who would believe me now, that I didn't kill the old crone? I will be caught this very same day, either right here or back in the city, at the train station, like that gent who was being led off, with his head bowed low.

I step out into the car's vestibule. The train is approaching Lisy Nos. The white mileposts by the side of the road are flashing by. The train comes to a stop. The steps down from my train car do not reach the ground. I hop off and walk toward the station pavilion. It is another half an hour until the train returning to the city.

✦

I enter a sparse grove. There are scrubby bushes of juniper there. No one will see me behind them. I head for the bushes.

A large green caterpillar is crawling on the earth. I get down on my knees and touch it with my fingers. It spasms and convulses muscularly, contracting several times, first in one direction then in the other.

I look around. No one sees me here. A light shiver runs down my spine.

I bow my head down and pronounce under my breath:

"In the name of the Father, the Son, and the Holy Spirit, now and forever, till the end of times. Amen."

✦

At this point, I must temporarily break off my manuscript, considering as I do that it has gone on far too long already.

[*May–June 1939*]

An Innoculation

A gentleman slight in height with a pebble in his eye approached the door of a tobacco shop and stopped there. His polished black shoes shone by the stone steps leading up into the tobacco shop. The tips of the shoes were pointing inside the shop. Two more steps and the gentleman would have disappeared behind its door.

But for some reason he tarried, as if intentionally, to place his head under the brick that had just fallen off the roof. The gentleman even removed his hat, as if only now discovering his bald skull, so that the brick hit the gentleman squarely on his naked head, breaking his skull bone and getting stuck in his brain.

The gentleman did not fall down. No, he only swooned from the terrible blow and, removing a handkerchief from his pocket, wiped his face . . . And, turning toward the crowd, which had at once gathered around this gentleman, he said:

Don't worry, gentlemen, I've already had an inoculation. You see, the pebble sticking out of my right eye? This had happened to me once already. I've gotten used to it by now. It's all a piece of cake now.

And with these words the gentleman put on his hat and went off somewhere, exiting stage right, leaving the confused crowd in complete bewilderment.

[*1939–40*]

It was summertime . . .

It was summertime. The sun was shining. It was very hot. A hammock hung in the garden. In the hammock sat a little boy named Plato.

Plato sat in the hammock, swinging back and forth, squinting from the sun.

Suddenly something peered out at him from behind the lilac bush and then hid again.

Plato wanted to get up and see what it was, but climbing out of the hammock was difficult. The hammock swung and creaked pleasantly, the butterflies fluttered and the bees buzzed all around him. The kerosene stove hissed inside the house. Plato stayed in the hammock, rocking back and forth.

From behind the lilac bush something once again peered out and then hid.

"It must be our pussycat, Zhenka," Plato thought.

And indeed, from behind the bush emerged a cat, but it wasn't Zhenka. Zhenka was gray with white spots, and this one was all gray, without any spots.

"Where did this cat come from?" Plato wondered. And then he noticed that the pussycat was wearing glasses. And not just that: the pussycat had a little pipe in its mouth and was puffing on it.

Plato, his eyes wide open, stared at the pussycat. And the pussycat, seeing Plato, approached him and, taking the pipe out of its mouth, said:

"Please forgive me! You wouldn't happen to know where around here lives Plato?"

"That's me," Plato said.

"Oh, it is you?" the pussycat said. "In that case, would you please follow me, behind this bush? A certain somebody wishes to meet you."

Plato extracted himself from the hammock and followed the cat. Behind the bush, balancing on one leg, stood a heron.

Seeing Plato, the heron flapped her wings, swung her head, and made a clicking noise with her beak.

"Greetings!" said the heron and extended its foot to Plato.

Plato, wanting to shake the heron's foot, held out his hand.

"Don't you dare!" the pussycat said. "Handshakes have been forbidden! If you wish to exchange greetings, you must do so with your feet!"

Plato stretched out his leg and touched the heron's foot with his own foot.

"That's good, now you're acquainted," the pussycat said.

"Arethen Letusfry!" the heron said.

"Yes, let us fly!" said the pussycat and jumped on the heron's back.

"Fly where?" Plato asked. But the heron had already snagged him by the back of his neck and taken off.

"Let me go!" Plato screamed.

"Nonsense!" the pussycat said, sitting on the heron's back. "If we let go of you, you will fall and die."

Plato looked down and saw the roof of his house.

"Where are we going?" Plato asked.

"Over there," the pussycat said, flapping his paws in all directions at once.

Plato looked down once again and saw below him the gardens, the streets, and the tiny houses. Several people stood on the town square and, shading their eyes with their hands, gazed up at the sky.

"Save me!" Plato yelled.

"Sirence!" the heron screamed, opening its beak wide.

Plato felt something constricting in his chest and heard a deafening noise in his ears, and the square with the tiny people began to grow quickly.

And then Plato heard the pussycat's voice above him: "Catch him! He's falling!"

[*late 1930s*]

Knights (A House Full of Old Women)

There was a house full of old women. The old women stumbled about the house all day and swatted flies with rolled-up newspaper cones. Altogether in the house there were thirty-six of them.

The most spirited of the old women, by the name of Yufleva, bossed around the rest of them.

When the old women disobeyed, she would pinch them on their upper arms or stick her foot out to trip them, and they would fall and split their ugly mugs. The old woman Zvyakina, punished by Yufleva, fell so awkwardly that she broke both of her jaws. They had to call in a doctor. The man came, put on a dressing gown, and, having examined Zvyakina, said that she is far too old to count on her jaws healing. After which the doctor requested to be given a little hammer, a chisel, pliers, and a length of rope. The old women raced around the house for some time, not knowing what pliers and a chisel looked like, and kept bringing the doctor everything that seemed to them to resemble these instruments. The doctor kept cursing, but finally, having been brought the requested items, asked everyone to remove themselves from the premises. The old women, burning with curiosity, departed, mumbling under their breath in great displeasure. "Let's see," the doctor said and, grabbing Zvyakina, tied her up with the rope. Then the doctor, paying no attention to Zvyakina's loud screams and protestations, applied the chisel to her jaw and struck it with the hammer. Zvyakina began to groan in a hoarse, low baritone. Having pulverized Zvyakina's jaws with the chisel, the doctor grabbed the pliers and pulled Zvyakina's jaws out. Zvyakina howled, groaned, and, growing hoarse, drenched herself in blood. And the doctor, having tossed the pliers with Zvyakina's extracted jaws on the floor, took off the dressing gown, wiped his hands with it, walked over to the door, and swung it open. Squealing, the old women tumbled into the room and, their eyes bulging out, stared, some at Zvyakina, some at the bloody fragments scattered around the floor. The doctor elbowed his way through the crowd of old women and took his leave. The old women swarmed around Zvyakina. Zvyakina grew silent and, by the looks of it, commenced dying. Yufleva stood nearby, studying Zvyakina over while chomping on sunflower seeds. The old woman Byashechina said: "See here, Yufleva, one day we too shall lie down to our eternal rest." Yufleva tried to kick Byashechina, but the other one had time to jump out of the way.

"Let us go, old women!" said Byashechina. "There's nothing for us to do here. Let Yufleva putter around with Zvyakina, and we can go on swatting flies."

And the old women hoofed it toward the door.

Yufleva, still spitting out the sunflower seed husks, stood in the middle of the room staring at Zvyakina. Zvyakina stopped whimpering and was lying perfectly still. Perhaps she was now dead.

Whatever the case may be, on this point, the author must conclude his narrative, as he is unable to locate his inkwell.

♀ [*Friday*] *June 21, 1940*

A Genuine Lover of Nature

. . . he breathes in through his mouth and expands his stomach, until it begins to hurt under the clavicles. And now he descends from the bridge and crosses the fields. Now he sees a delicate flower and, getting down on all fours, smells and kisses it. Now he lies down upon the earth and listens to some sort of rustling. He crawls on the ground, without a care for his clothes. He crawls and cries out in happiness. He is overjoyed, for his nature is of the earth.

A genuine lover of nature is always smelling the least bit signs of nature. Even in the city, staring at the expressionless mug of a horse, he sees endless steppes, thornbush, and dust, and his ears are full of cowbells. He, squeezing his eyes closed, shakes his head and now no longer knows if he is a horse or a person. He neighs, stomps his hoof, swings his imaginary tail, bares his horse teeth, and, in the manner of a horse, taints the wind.

May God spare me a meeting with such a genuine lover of nature.

[*1939–40*]

An Obstacle

Pronin said, "You have very pretty stockings."

Irina Mazer said, "So you like my stockings?"

Pronin said, "Oh, yes. Very much." And he ran his hand down her leg.

Irina said, "But what do you like about my stockings?"

Pronin said, "They are very smooth."

Irina lifted her skirt and said, "Do you see how high they go?"

Pronin said, "Oh, yes. Yes."

Irina said, "They end all the way up here. And there, I am nude."

"Oh," said Pronin.

"I have very thick legs," said Irina. "And I'm very broad in the thighs."

"Show me," said Pronin.

"I can't," said Irina. "I'm not wearing any underwear."

Pronin knelt on his knees before her.

Irina said, "Why did you get down to your knees?"

Pronin kissed her leg just above the stocking and said, "Here's why."

Irina said, "Why are you lifting my skirt? Didn't I tell you that I'm not wearing any underwear?"

But Pronin lifted her skirt anyway and said, "That's alright."

"What do you mean by that, alright?" Irina said.

At that moment someone knocked on the door of Irina's room. Irina quickly righted her skirt. Pronin got up off the floor and went to stand by the window.

"Who is it?" Irina asked at the door.

"Open the door," a voice commanded.

Irina opened the door, and in walked a man wearing a black coat and high boots. Behind him were two soldiers, armed with rifles, and the apartment super. The soldiers guarded the door, and the man in the black coat approached Irina Mazer and said, "Your last name?"

"Mazer," Irina said.

The man in the black coat addressed Pronin: "Your last name?"

Pronin said, "Pronin. My last name is Pronin."

"Are you armed?" said the man in the black coat.

"No," Pronin said.

"Sit here," said the man in the black coat, pointing to a chair.

Pronin sat down.

"And you," said the man in the black coat, addressing Irina, "put on your coat. You will have to take a ride with us."

"What for?" Irina asked.

The man in the black coat didn't reply.

"I have to change," Irina said.

"No," said the man in the black coat.

"But I have to put on a little something," said Irina.

"No," said the man in the black coat.

Irina silently grabbed her fur jacket.

"Good-bye," she said to Pronin.

"Conversation is forbidden," said the man in the black coat.

"Do I have to go with you also?" Pronin asked.

"Yes," said the man in the black coat. "Get your coat."

Pronin got up, grabbed his coat and hat off the hanger, put them on, and said, "Alright, I'm ready."

"Follow me," said the man in the black coat.

The soldiers and the apartment super clicked their heels.

Everyone exited into the hallway.

The man in the black coat locked the door to Irina's room and sealed it with two brown seals.

"Everybody out," he said.

And they all walked out of the house, slamming the apartment door shut.

August 12, 1940

Perechin [Mr. Contrarian]

Perechin sat on a thumbtack, and from that moment on his life changed abruptly. From a quiet, thoughtful person, Perechin turned into a confirmed mischief-maker. He let his mustache grow out and subsequently trimmed it in such a careless way that one side of his mustache was always longer than the other. And besides, his mustache grew in a very uneven way, so that it became unpleasant to even look at Perechin. And to boot, he winked his eyes and twisted his cheeks in a disturbing manner. For quite some time Perechin limited himself to minor delinquencies: he spread rumors, wrote denunciations, and shortchanged the women train conductors, paying them for the ride with the smallest copper coins and always omitting two and sometimes even three kopeks.

August 14, 1940

How easy it is for a man to become lost in insignificant details . . .

How easy it is for a man to become lost in insignificant details. It is possible to pace for hours from the table to the wardrobe and from the wardrobe to the sofa without finding the exit. It is even possible to forget one's whereabouts and shoot arrows at some small case suspended from the wall. "Hey, you!" you can yell at it, "I'm gonna get you!" Or one can lie down on the floor beholding closely the specks of dust. This too contains inspiration. It is best to do this for hours, having come to terms with time. Of course, it is very difficult to determine a schedule for this, for what sort of time frame does dust have?

It is better still to gaze into a basin of water. Gazing into water is always beneficial and instructive. Even if there is nothing to see in it, at least it always feels good. We gazed into the water, saw nothing in it, and very quickly became quite bored. But we soothed ourselves with the notion that we were after all doing something beneficial. We folded our fingers into our fists, and counted them. But we had no idea what it was we were counting, for what is it that could possibly be enumerated in water?

August 17, 1940

A Lecture

Pushkov said:

"A woman is the lathe of love."

And he immediately got punched in the face.

"What for?" Pushkov asked.

But, not receiving an answer to his question, he went on:

"This is my thought: a woman should be approached from underneath. Women find this endearing and only give the impression that they don't like it."

Then Pushkov got another one in the teeth.

"What's going on here, comrade!? If this goes on, I'll stop speaking altogether," said Pushkov.

But, having waited a quarter of a minute, he continued.

"A woman's constructed so that she's all soft and moist."

Pushkov got punched in the face again, but this time he tried to act as if nothing had happened and continued.

"If you are to smell a woman . . ."

But this time he got smacked so hard that he grabbed his cheek and said:

"It is entirely impossible to deliver a lecture under such circumstances. If this is repeated, I will quit."

Pushkov waited another quarter of a minute and then went on:

"So, where were we? Oh yes! As I was saying, a woman loves to admire herself. She sits down in front of a mirror completely naked . . ."

At this word, he once again got smacked in the mouth.

"Naked," Pushkov repeated.

Smack! he got walloped again.

"Naked!" Pushkov yelled.

Smack! another wallop.

"Naked! The woman is naked! A naked dame!" Pushkov yelled.

Smack! Smack! Smack! he got pummeled again and again and again.

"A naked dame with a pitcher in her hands!" Pushkov yelled.

Smack! Smack! punches were now raining down upon Pushkov.

"A woman's tail!" Pushkov screamed, evading the blows. "Naked nun!"

But then Pushkov got hit so hard that he lost his consciousness and collapsed to the floor as though he had been mowed down.

[*1940*]

The Descent (Nearby and Far Away)

Two men fell off a roof. They both fell off the roof of a five-story building, a new construction. A school, I think. They slid down the roof in a sitting position to the very edge and then they started falling. Ida Markovna saw them falling before anyone else. She was standing in the window of the building on the opposite side of the street and blowing her nose into a glass. Then suddenly she saw that someone was beginning to fall from the roof of the building across the way. Looking closely, Ida Markovna saw that it was two people at once who were beginning to fall. Completely stunned, Ida Markovna stripped the shirt off her back and with this shirt began to rub the steamed-up glass of the window so that she could see more clearly who it was that was falling from the roof. However, realizing that in their turn those falling may well see her naked and think God knows what, Ida Markovna jumped away from the window and hid behind a woven planter that at some point in time had held a flowerpot. At this time, a different personage living in the same house as Ida Markovna, only two floors below her, also saw the two people falling. This personage was also named Ida Markovna. It just so happened that at the same time she was sitting with her feet up on the sill, sewing a buckle onto her shoe. Looking up out of the window, she saw the two people falling. Ida Markovna let out a squeal and, jumping up from the windowsill, began to open the window so that she could see better how the people falling from the roof would hit the ground. But the window would not open. Ida Markovna remembered that she had nailed the bottom of the window shut and immediately ran to the fireplace in which she kept her tools: four hammers, a chisel, and pliers. Grabbing the pliers, Ida Markovna ran back to the window and pulled out the nail. Now the window opened easily. Ida Markovna stuck her head out of the window and saw how the people falling from the roof were flying down toward the ground with a whistling sound.

A small crowd had already collected in the street. People were already letting out whistles and, approaching unhurriedly toward the expected location of the event, was a policeman of very short stature. A long-nosed street sweeper was fussily pushing the people who had gathered away with his elbows, explaining to them that the two falling from the roof might land on their heads. By this time, both of the Ida Markovnas, the one in a dress and the one naked, their heads sticking out of the windows, were already squealing and kicking up their feet in excitement. And so, finally, the two men falling from the roof, their hands spread out to brace themselves and their eyes bulging wide open, hit the ground.

Just as we sometimes, falling from the heights of our realized accomplishments, smash against the depressing prison of our existence.

composed over a period of four days
completed on ♄ [*Saturday*] *7* ♍ [*September*] *1940*

The Power Of

Faol said: "We sin and perform good deeds blindly. A short-order cook was riding a bicycle and suddenly, having passed the Kazan Cathedral, he vanished. Was he even aware of what it is he was supposed to have accomplished: either good or evil? Or this case: an artist bought himself a fur coat and, as it were, performed a good deed for that old woman who, in her need, was obliged to sell this fur coat, but to another old lady, and namely his own mother, who lived with the artist and regularly slept in the hallway where the artist hung his new coat, he caused, from all appearances, an evil, for as a result of the new fur, which stunk so unbearably of formaldehyde or naphthalene, the old woman, the mother of the artist, was once unable to wake up and croaked. Or the following case: one graphic artist got so loaded with vodka and made such a mess that, one might say, even the Captain Dibich himself would not have been able to distinguish what was good and what evil. It is immensely difficult to distinguish sin from goodness."

Mouseman [Myshin], having become mesmerized in thought by Faol's words, fell out of his chair.

Wow, he said, lying on the floor. Wha wha?

Faol continued: "Take, for example, love. It may be for better or for worse. On the one hand, it is written: you must love . . . but on the other hand, it is said: do not spoil . . . Perhaps it is better not to love after all? But it says: you must love. But if you do love, you will spoil. What to do? Perhaps go ahead and love but in some other way? But then why is it that in all languages, the same word is used to designate both this and the other love? So, this one artist loved his mother and this one plump young girl. And he loved them each differently. He handed over to the girl the larger part of his salary. The mother often starved while the girl ate and drank for three people. The artist's mother slept in the hallway on the floor, and the girl had at her disposure two very adequate rooms. The girl had four coats and the mother just one. And so, the artist took from his mother her one coat and had it altered into a skirt for the girl. So that, in all respects, the artist spoiled the girl but his own mother he didn't spoil, but loved her with a pure love. However, he did fear his mother's death, but the death of the girlfriend he feared not, and when his mother died, the artist cried, and when the girlfriend fell out of a window and also died, the artist didn't cry but found himself another girlfriend. And so it seems that a mother is prized as one of a kind, as though she were a rare stamp that cannot be replaced with another."

Que-que, said Mouseman, lying on the floor. Wow.

Faol continued: "And this is what is called pure love! Is such love kind? And if not, then how must one love? One mother loved her child. This child was two and a half years old. The mother carried the child to a playground and placed him in a sandbox. Other mothers brought their children to the same sandbox. At times, as many as forty children were collected in this sandbox. And so, one time, a rabid dog burst into this playground and pounced on the children and began biting them. The mothers, including our mother, howling, flung themselves on their children. She, sacrificing herself, grabbed the dog and pulled out of its jaws—or so it seemed to her—her own child. But, having rescued the child, she realized it wasn't her child after all, and the mother tossed the child back to bait the dog in order to grab and save from certain death her own child, lying there beside the other. Who will tell me: did she commit a sin or did she perform a good deed?"

Come again, said Mouseman, squirming on the floor.

Faol continued: "Does the stone sin? Is a tree evil? Is an animal contemptible? Or is it man alone who sins?"

Toodle-oodle, said Mouseman, listening attentively to Faol's words. Shup-shup.

Faol continued: "If man alone sins, then it means that all the world's sins are concentrated in man himself. Sin does not per se enter the man but only emerges out of him. Just as with food: a man eats what is good and expels the bad out of himself. The world itself contains nothing bad, besides that which has been digested by man; only that which has passed through man may become bad."

Shmartyful, said Mouseman, trying to raise himself up off the floor.

Faol continued: "And so I was speaking of love. I was speaking of those human conditions that we designate by the one word, 'love.' Is this an error of semantics, or are all these conditions as one? The mother's love for her child, the son's love for his mother, and the love of a man for a woman—can all these be one love?"

Most definitely! said Mouseman, nodding his head.

Faol said, "Yes, I believe the essence of love does not change depending on who loves or who is loved. Each person is allotted a predetermined quantity of love. And each person searches out where it may be applied, without throwing off one's mortal coil. The revelation of the mysteries of the transmutations and the trivial qualities of our souls, it is akin to a bag of sawdust . . ."

Nuff! screamed Mouseman, jumping up from the floor. Be gone!

And Faol dissolved, like a cube of surplus sugar.

⊙ [*Sunday*] *29* ♎ [*September*] *1940*

A certain graphologist who loved vodka ...

A certain graphologist who loved vodka excessively sat on the bench in the garden and thought how pleasant it would be to enter now into a spacious room in which lives a large and lovely family with young daughters who play on the grand piano. They would greet the graphologist lovingly and show him to the dining room and seat him in an armchair by the fireplace and place before him a small table. And standing on the table would be a carafe of vodka and a plate of hot fried meat dumplings. The graphologist would sit there and drink vodka, chasing each shot with a bite of the hot dumplings, and the family's pretty daughters would be playing on the grand piano in the neighboring room and singing beautiful arias out of Italian operas.

[*1940*]

All people love money . . .

All people love money. They pat it and kiss it and press it to their hearts and wrap it in pretty strips of cloth and cradle and rock it as though it were a doll. Some take a dollar sign and confine it to a frame, hang it on their wall, and worship it as though it were an icon or an idol. Some feed their money: they open its mouth and stuff it with the most succulent, fat morsels of their own food. In summer heat they put their money in the cold storage of a root cellar and in winter, in the bittermost frost, they throw the money in the wood stove, into the flames. Others simply hold a conversation with their money, or read to it aloud from interesting books, or sing to it pleasant songs. I personally give money no particular attention and simply carry it around in my wallet or in a billfold and, as need arises, spend it. Yowza!

October 16, 1940

The Good Doctor

On the bed, writhing in pain, lay a young man, translucent to the point of disappearing. On the chair sat a woman, likely his mother, covering her face with her hands. A gentleman wearing a starched collar, probably a doctor, stood beside the nightstand. Yellow drapes were drawn over the windows. The door creaked, and a large tomcat peeked into the room. The gentleman in the starched collar kicked the cat on the nose with his boot. The cat vanished. The young man moaned.

The young man said something. The doctor-like gentleman listened. The young man said, "The boats are sailing." The gentleman bent forward.

"How are you, my dear friend?" the gentleman asked, leaning closer. The young man lay silently on his back, his face turned to the wall.

He remained silent.

"Alright, then," the gentleman said, straightening. "You refuse to speak to your friend. Fine."

The gentleman shrugged and moved to the window.

"Give me a boat," the young man said.

The gentleman, standing by the window, snickered.

***

Eight minutes passed. The youth fixed his eyes on the gentleman in the starched collar and said, "Doctor, please tell me honestly, am I dying?"

"See here," the doctor said, fingering the chain of his pocket watch, "I'd rather not answer your question. Indeed, I don't even have the right to answer it."

"What you just said is plenty," the young man said. "I know now that there's no hope."

"You're just imagining," said the doctor. "I didn't say anything of the sort about hope."

"Doctor, you must take me for a fool. But I assure you, I'm not stupid and I understand my condition perfectly."

The doctor snickered and shrugged.

"Your condition is such," he said, "that it would be impossible for you to understand it."

[*1940*]

One man was chasing another . . .

One man was chasing another, and the one running away was, in his turn, chasing a third one who, unaware he was being chased, was simply striding along on the pavement stones at a moderate pace.

[*1940*]

The Adventures of Mr. Caterpillar

Mishurin was a caterpillar. Because of this, or perhaps for another reason, he loved to wallow under the sofa or behind the dresser, sucking in the dust. Because he was a somewhat slovenly person, sometimes for an entire day his mug would be covered in dust, as though with eiderdown.

Once upon a time he was invited as a guest to someone's house, and Mishurin decided to give his countenance a light rinse. He filled a bowl with lukewarm water and added some vinegar to it and immersed his face in this water. As it turns out, this mixture contained too much vinegar, and for the rest of his long life Mishurin was blind. Into his deep old age, he walked around feeling his way about with his hands, and for this reason, or perhaps another, he came to resemble a caterpillar even more.

♀ *[Friday] October 16, 1940*

The streets were becoming immersed in silence . . .

The streets were becoming immersed in silence. At the intersections, people stood waiting for trolley buses. Some of them, having given up hope, set off on foot. And so at one of these intersections, on the Petrograd side of town, only two people remained. One of them was particularly short in stature, with a round face and protruding ears. The other was slightly taller and, as was apparent, lame in his left foot. They were not acquainted with each other, but their common interest in the trolley bus forced them into conversing. The conversation was initiated by the lame man.

I don't know what to do, he said, as though directing himself to no one. It's probably not even worth waiting here.

The round-faced man turned toward the lame one and said:

I don't think so, it might still come.

[*1940*]

Mob Justice

Petrov saddles up his horse and declaims, directing himself at the crowd that's gathered round, what would happen if in place of the public gardens they erect an American skyscraper. The crowd seems to agree. Petrov scribbles something into his notebook. From the throng emerges a man of medium height and he asks Petrov what it was he jotted down. Petrov answers that it concerns no one but himself. The man of medium height continues to pester him and, after words are exchanged, they come to blows. The crowd allies itself with the man of medium height and Petrov has to save his life by flogging his horse and disappearing around a corner. The crowd surges with anxiety and, having no one to sacrifice, grabs the man of medium height and cracks his head open. The decapitated head rolls down the bridge paving stones and becomes wedged in the sewer drain. The crowd, its lust for violence appeased, disperses.

[*1940*]

Northern Fable

An old man, for no particular reason, went off, into the forest. Then he returned and said: Old woman, hey, old woman!

And the old woman dropped dead. Ever since then, all rabbits are white in winter.

[*1940*]

Mouseman's [Myshin's] Victory

Mouseman [Myshin] was told: "Hey, Mouseman, get up!"

Mouseman said, "I won't," and continued to lie on the floor.

Then Kalugin approached Mouseman and said, "If you, Mouseman, don't get up, I will force you to get up."

"No," said Mouseman, continuing to lie on the floor.

Selizneova approached Mouseman and said, "You, Mouseman, are always sprawled on the floor in the corridor, blocking us from walking there and back."

"I have been blocking you and will continue to block you," said Mouseman.

"You know what," said Korshunov [Vultureman], but Kalugin interrupted him and said:

"There's no point going on with this conversation. Call the police."

They rang the police and asked for a policeman to come.

Half an hour later, the policeman came in with the apartment super.

"What's going on here?" asked the policeman.

"Take a look at this," said Korshunov, but Kalugin interrupted him and said:

"See here. This citizen lies here on the floor all the time and does not allow us to use the corridor. We've tried this and that . . ."

Here Kalugin was interrupted by Selizneova who said:

"We have asked him to leave but he refuses."

"Yes," said Korshunov.

The policeman approached Mouseman.

"You, citizen, why are you lying there?" the policeman asked.

"I'm resting," said Mouseman.

"This is not the right place for resting, citizen," said the policeman. "Where do you live, citizen?"

"Here," said Mouseman.

"Where is your room?" asked the policeman.

"He is assigned to our apartment, but he doesn't have a room," said Kalugin.

"Please wait, citizen," said the policeman. "I will have a talk with him now. Citizen, where do you sleep?"

"Here," said Mouseman.

"May I," said Korshunov, but Kalugin interrupted him and said:

"He doesn't even have a bed and lies around here right on the bare floor."

"They have been complaining about him a long time," said the apartment super.

"It's completely impossible to walk around in the corridor," said Selizneova. "I can't be having to step over some man all the time. And he intentionally stretches out his feet, and his hands to boot, and lies on his back looking up from below me. And I come home from work tired, I have to rest."

"I would add that," said Korshunov, but he was immediately interrupted by Kalugin, who said:

"He lies here even at night. Everyone trips over him in the dark. I snagged my blanket over him and it ripped."

Selizneova said: "All sorts of nails are always falling out of his pockets. It's impossible to walk around the apartment in bare feet, or you might just impale yourself."

"Not too long ago they wanted to set him on fire with kerosene," said the apartment super.

"We soaked him with kerosene," said Korshunov, but Kalugin interrupted him and said:

"We only soaked him in kerosene to give him a scare; we never intended to set him on fire."

"I would never allow someone alive to be set on fire in my presence," said Selizneova.

"Why is this citizen lying in the corridor?" the policeman suddenly asked.

"Hello there!" said Korshunov, but Kalugin interrupted him and said:

"It's because he doesn't have an allotted living space; I live in this room here, in that, those over there, in that, this one here, and Mouseman, well, he lives here in the corridor."

"This isn't right," said the policeman. "Everyone ought to lie down in the room assigned to him."

"But he doesn't have any other room, just here in the corridor," said Kalugin.

"Precisely," said Korshunov.

"That's why he's always lying here," said Selizneova.

"This isn't right," said the policeman, and he walked away together with the apartment super.

Korshunov ran over to Mouseman.

"There!" he yelled at him. "How did you like that?!"

"Hold on a minute," said Kalugin. And, walking over to Mouseman, he said:

"Did you hear what the policeman said? Get up off the floor!"

"I won't get up," said Mouseman, continuing to lie on the floor.

"Now he will do it out of spite, and he'll lie here forever," said Selizneova.

"That's for sure," said Kalugin in frustration.

And Korshunov added:

"I am certain of it. Parfaitement!"

☌ [*Tuesday*] 8 ♏ [*October or November*] 1940

The Conversationalists

On the tram sat two men engaged in the following conversation. One was saying: "I do not believe in life after death. No substantial evidence exists that life after death exists. No such authoritative testimony is known to us. And in religions also, it is mentioned either not particularly convincingly, as in Islam, or quite nebulously, as, for example, in Christianity, or it is not mentioned at all, as in the Bible, or it is directly said not to exist, as in Buddhism. The instances of visions, prophecies, various miracles, and even accounts which relate direct experiences of life beyond the grave neither possess nor may serve as definitive proof of its existence. I am not interested one jot in such tales, like the one about a man who saw a lion in his dream and the next day was killed by a lion escaped from the zoological exhibit. I am only interested in one question: does life after death exist or does it not? Tell me, what are your thoughts on the subject?"

The second Conversationalist said: "This is my answer to you: you will never get an answer to your question, and if you ever do get an answer, you will not believe it. Only you will be able to answer this question. If you answer yes, then it will be yes, if you answer no, then it will be no. Only one must answer with complete conviction, without the shadow of a doubt, or, speaking more precisely, with complete faith in your answer."

The first Conversationalist said: "I would gladly answer myself. Yet it must be answered faithfully. But to answer with faith, one must be sure in the truth of one's answer. And where can I possibly find such certainty?"

The second Conversationalist replied: "Certainty or, more precisely, faith cannot be acquired, it can only be developed in oneself."

The first Conversationalist answered: "How can I possibly develop in myself faith in my own answer, when I don't even know how I should answer, yes or no?"

The second Conversationalist said: "Choose for yourself that answer which suits you best."

"Our stop is coming up," the first Conversationalist said, and both men got up out of their seats in order to move toward the exit.

"I am sorry to interrupt," a military man of extraordinary height addressed them. "I overheard your conversation and, forgive me, but I was wondering: how could two still relatively young men in all earnestness be speaking of this, of life after death, whether it exists or not?"

[*1940*]

Symphony No. 2

Anton Mikhailovich spat, said "akh," spat again, said "akh" again, spat again, again said "akh," and left. Well, to hell with him. I'll tell you about Ilya Pavlovich instead.

Ilya Pavlovich was born in 1883 in Constantinople. When he was still a little boy he was brought to Petersburg, and here he completed the German School on Kirochnaya Street. Then he worked in some sort of a store, then he did something else for a while, and at the start of the revolution he emigrated abroad. Well, to hell with him. I will tell you about Anna Ignatievna instead.

But to tell you about Anna Ignatievna isn't so simple. First of all, I know practically nothing about her and, second of all, I just fell off the stool and forgot what I was about to say. Better I tell you about myself.

I am tall in height, not stupid, dress colorfully and with taste, don't drink, don't patronize the horses, but do like the ladies. And the ladies do not avoid me. In fact, they love it when I accompany them. Seraphima Izmailovna has invited me time and again over to her place, and Zinaida Yakovlevna also told me that she is always happy to see me. And with Marina Petrovna I had this amusing episode, which is the one I want to tell you about. The episode is really quite ordinary, but still very amusing, because Marina Petrovna turned, owing to me, entirely bald, like the palm of your hand. It happened this way: I came over to Marina Petrovna's and she "boom!" turned completely bald. That's it.

June 9–11, 1941

A Young Man Who Had
Surprised the Night Watchman

What have we got here, said the guard, inspecting a fly. If you only slather wood glue over it, it would likely be the end of him. How's that for a story! From simple glue!

Hey, you, ogre! a young man wearing yellow gloves hailed the night watchman.

The watchman realized immediately that his attention was required but continued examining the fly.

I'm talking to you! the young man screamed once more. You dumbass!

The watchman squashed the fly with his thumb and, without turning his head to the young man, said:

And you, shit-for-brains, what are you yelling for? I can hear you. There ain't no need to raise your voice!

The young man wiped his gloves on his pants and delicately asked, pointing to the sky:

Would you please tell me, grandpa, how do I get up there?

The watchman looked the young man over, squinted in one eye, then squinted in the other, then scratched his little goatee, looked the young man over one more time, and said:

Well, there's no reason to loiter here, go on, keep going, sonny.

Forgive me, the young man said, but I am here on an urgent matter. They've even prepared a room for me here.

Alrighty, said the watchman, show me your ticket.

I don't have it with me. They said that I'd be let through without it, the young man said, looking attentively into the watchman's eyes.

Ain't that something! the watchman said.

So, what will it be? asked the young man. Will you let me through?

Alright, alright, said the watchman. You can go in.

And how do I get there from here? Where do I go? the young man asked. I don't know the way.

Where do you need to go? asked the watchman, fixing him with a severe expression.

The young man covered his mouth with his palm and said very quietly:

To the sky!

The watchman leaned forward, shifted his right foot so as to stand more firmly, fixed the young man in his sights, and in a severe voice asked:

You're a wise guy? Are you pulling my leg?

The young man smiled, raised his hand, clad in a yellow glove, waved it above his head, and suddenly disappeared.

The watchman sniffed the air. The air smelled of singed feathers.

How about that! the watchman said, swung his coat open, scratched his stomach, spat on the place where the young man had been standing, and slowly walked back to his booth.

[date unknown]

Selected Poems

✦ 1927–1939 ✦

I am interested only in pure nonsense, only in that which has no practical meaning. I am interested in life only in its absurd manifestation. I find heroics, pathos, moralizing, all that is hygienic and tasteful abhorrent . . . both as words and as feelings.
—Daniil Kharms, October 31, 1937

Society of Friends of Chamber Music

do not attend in January
say sometime around nine
performing is the Left Flank
it is simply terrible
in fact it's a flop

January 1927

* * *

To A. I. Vvedensky

My friend fell in a laughable tub
The wall dizzily circling around
A beautiful cow floated about
Above the house the street babbled
And my friend flickering on the sand
Paced the rooms in his bare socks
Twiddling like a conjurer his hands
First the left and then the other
Then diving on his unmade bed
Like in the swamps the weed-wets
Made bird sounds with his hat and howled
My friend who was no longer in the bath

March 5, 1927

* * *

You can sew. But that's all bunk.
I'm in love with your pudenda;
it's moist and smells abundantly.
Another man would peek, let out
a squeak, and, sealing his nose, scram.
And wiping your fluids from his hands
would he return? Oh, what a question;
suddenly, there can be no other.
Your juices are to me sheer joy.
You think my words are an excrescence
but I'm prepared to lick your cunt
without break for breath and swallow
the delicious squim of your mallow
until I begin to burp and grunt.

[*1931*]

In the Name of the Father, the Son, and the Holy Ghost
yesterday I sat by the window hanging an ear out
and the earth was saying to the tree: grow strong
the tree grew slowly—still visible to the naked eye
at times undressed or hiding its trunk in a green
vase reading on the sun the sign of its happiness
occasionally the planets shivered among the stars
and the tree flapped flexing with its bird nests
some seven rainbows sprouted above the tree
I saw the icons of the angel's eyes
they gazed upon us down from above
reading off the dear days of the calendar

[*1931*]

* * *

Seated at a table, flighty thoughts,
shoulders spread, inflated chest,
I pronounced empty speeches,
still as a statue and just as loved.

[*1930–33?*]

* * *

The wise are guided in a split sec.
The foolish know it all from books.
A wise man and a fool are no pair,
The wise, cargo, the fool a container.

[*1933*]

* * *

Before me hangs a portrait
of Alice Ivanovna Poret.
She is as gorgeous as a fairy,
devious, worse than a snake,
she is cunning, my Alice,
cunning as Renard the Fox.

[*January 7, 1933*]

* * *

Entering the grand, magnificent
House of the Central Soviets,
with her mouth wide agape,
walked in my dear Elizabeth.

[*September 1933*]

* * *

Having slammed the tome shut
I sat all day with an open mouth.
Having read all of fifteen lines
I suddenly became toward life unkind.

[*September 1933*]

* * *

Dear manager, I need money
To take a trip to the baths.
But, without a buck, I can't
Even buy myself a sponge.

[*mid-1930s*]

* * *

Then even a wife will not save you
in the insanity of her jealous ways
nor the allures of beloved leisure
nor the sweet celebrations of holidays.

[*mid-1930s*]

* * *

Immersed in their thoughts people scram.
Where are they rushing? Why do they run?
The women are swishing their breasts around.
The gentlemen's beards emit a rustling sound.

[*1933–36*]

The Permanence of Dirt and Rejoicing

The water gurgles coolly in the river,
the mountain's shadow falls upon the field,
and in the sky the light goes out. The birds
are flying now through visions in a dream.
The gardener with his black mustaches
stands still all night beneath the open gates
and scratches between his grubby clutches
the back of his head under a muddy cap.
We hear in windows shouts of joy escaping,
stomping of feet and clattering of glasses.

A day thus passes, then an entire week,
and then the fleeting years go flying by,
and people, arrayed in their orderly rows,
march into their graves and disappear.
And the gardener with his black mustaches
stands still for years beneath the open gates
and scratches between his grubby clutches
the back of his head under a muddy cap.
We hear in windows shouts of joy escaping,
stomping of feet and clattering of glasses.

The sun and moon, dwindling, have grown paler,
the constellations, each having changed its shape.
Motion itself has become more viscous,
and time's acquired the consistency of sand.
The gardener with his black mustaches
stands once again beneath the open gates
and scratches between his grubby clutches

the back of his head under a muddy cap.
We hear in windows shouts of joy escaping,
stomping of feet and clattering of glasses.

October 14, 1933

* * *

King of the universe,
dearest king of nature,
king who is nameless,
who hasn't even a definite frame,
come over to my house and
together we will down some vodka,
and stuff ourselves with meat,
and then discuss our acquaintances.
Perhaps your visit will bring me
the Lord on High's autograph,
and perhaps even your photograph
that I may better your portrait depict.

March 27, 1934

* * *

It is your part to god-create me (this a heavenly gift),
A heavenly gift, one ought to think, a sacred gift.
Yes, I am definitely very very very interesting
And even very very very very highly evolved.

How satisfying to write without missing a beat!
And then what I have written out loud to read.
Yes, this is a most pleasant way to pass the time
Whence at once participate both body and soul.

That's when I feel myself in the universe's stream.

[*1935*]

Chorus

A cuckoo sleeps in a tree
A lobster dreams under a rock
In the field lies a shepherdess
And the wind is a two-way street.

[*1935*]

* * *

Money is for saving time
people scrambling for a train
a bell begins to loudly hum
and the engine lets out steam
the track signal lifts its mug
and the train begins to speak
we can hear the steel's sad moan—
jangling of a car against car
and the nodding of the rails—
means the train's begun its run.
And the engine's breathing fast
a lady dozing hides her nose
a lamp sheds light upon the floor
a soldier sleeping—no he's not—
he only for the hundredth time
flings his glinting glance at her
willing that she look at him.
The lady gives her leg a stir.

January 1, 1935

Thoughts about a Girl

Arriving at Lipavsky's once by chance,
I noted only to myself, in silence,
How pleasant it is on that rare occasion
To be left alone, one-on-one with a girl.

And when she passes by aflutter,
As if on air, not a word do you utter;
And when with a knowledgeable hand
She makes contact—you understand.

And when she lightly, as though dancing,
Sliding her lovely foot across the floor,
Proceeds to offer her perky breast for
You to kiss—then it is impossible not

To shout out loud and lovingly blow
From her firm breast a mote of dust,
And recognize how touching your lips
To her youthful breast is pointless.

January 21, 1935

The Physicist Who Broke His Leg

Models of the universe in his hands,
a physicist is seen departing his gates.
Suddenly felled, his kneecaps collapse.
People come running to his aid.
Flashing joints of mechanical motion
a policeman is seen approaching.
Reciting the multiplication table
a young student tries to help him.
A beautiful lady with a handbag.
With a walking stick an old hag.
And the physicist is on his back.
He cannot walk, it seems he's stuck.

January 23, 1935

To Oleinikov

Conductor of numbers, friendship's snide mocker,
What's on your mind? Will you renew your diatribe?
Homer to you a lowlife and Goethe a silly sinner,
Dante you laughed at and only Bunin was your guide.

Your verses often humorous, often troubled, often not
At all funny but instead they saddened our hearts.
Often they even stirred our ire and contained no art.
Rushing headlong into the abyss of pettiness and rot.

Wait! Turn back! Where, with your cold and calculated
Thought, are you fleeing, forgetting the law of the crowd?
Whose chest was pierced by arrow so morose? Who's
Enemy to you, who friend? And where's your gravestone?

January 23, 1935

Nikolai Oleinikov, a children's poet, the author of "Beetle, the Anti-Semite," and the oldest member of OBERIU, was arrested July 3, 1937, and executed after several months of torture on November 24, 1937.

To an Anonymous Natasha

His glasses mended with a piece of string,
    a gray-haired old man, reading a book.
A candle's burning and the twilight air
    churns with its wind the riffling pages.
The old man, sighing, smooths out his hair
    and with the remnants of his teeth
Gnaws on a crusty piece of stale bread:
    his jaws make loud crunching sounds.

Sunrise that's been erasing the stars now
    extinguishes the Prospect's streetlights.
The woman tram conductor is arguing
    with a drunk already for the fifth time.
The Neva River's hack cough sinisterly-
    stirred is now strangling the old man.
And I am writing verses to Natasha
    without ever closing my light-filled eyes.

January 23, 1935

* * *

Lord, please feed me on your flesh so that
it awakens in me the need for Thy emergence.
Lord, give me of your sweet blood to drink
that it resurrect in me the spirit of my verse.

Lord, awaken in my soul Thy fiery flame.
Shine upon me the rays of Thy sun.
Scatter your golden sands at my feet,
That I may walk the pure path to Thy House.
Reward me with Thy Word, Dear Lord,
That it thunders when I praise Thy Kingdom Hall.
Dear Lord, alter the trodden track of my life,
That the train engine of Thy majesty may startle.
Unthrottle, Lord, the brakes of my inspiration.
Soothe me, Dear Lord, and water my heart
With the source of Thy divine imagination.

Mars Field, May 13, 1935

Variations [Among the Guests]

Among the guests, wearing a shirt only,
Stood Petrov, wholly immersed in thought.
The guests were silent. Above the fireplace
An iron thermometer hung suspended.
The guests were silent. Above the fireplace
Suspended hung a hunting horn and Petrov
Stood silent. The clock hammered out the time
And in the fireplace a whiplike flame crackled.
And the gravely serious guests stood silent.
Petrov stood likewise. The fireplace crackled
And the wall clock announced it was eight.
The iron thermometer shone and twinkled.
Among the guests, dressed in shirt only,
Petrov remained in place still lost in thought
And the guests remained silent. Suspended
Above the fireplace hung a hunting horn
The wall clock now mysteriously silent.
A little flame danced a joyous jig in the fireplace
And Petrov, immersed in thought, sat down
On a footstool. In the hallway, like a madman,
The doorbell suddenly spilled over with sound
And the English lock let out a loud crack.
Petrov jumped and the guests were also stirred.
The hunting horn blew out a trumpet note
And Petrov screaming, "Oh God, Dear God!"
Is felled. He's down on the floor, as though killed.
And the guests scurry and scuttle and cry.
Shaking out the iron thermometer to use
With whoops and yells they jump over Petrov

And carry through the doorway a terrible coffin.
And stuffing Petrov in this coffin they leave,
With yells and shouts: "He's done for. Let's go home."

August 15, 1936

Dream of Two Ladies in Blackface

Two ladies are asleep, or no, they're not
They're not asleep, or rather yes they are
Certainly asleep and they dream a dream
As though Ivan's coming through the door
And, after Ivan, the building manager
Holding in his arms Tolstoy's volume
Of *War and Peace*, the second tome . . .
Or rather not, it's not that at all,
Tolstoy walks in and hangs his coat,
Takes off his galoshes and his boots,
And yells out, "Vanka! Give me a hand."
That's when Ivan grabs hold of an ax
And gives Tolstoy a whack on the back.
Tolstoy falls to the floor. What a disgrace!
All of Russian literature is a chamber pot.

August 19, 1936

* * *

A quiet evening thus descends on us
The bare light bulb casting an eerie sheen
The dogs beyond the walls are silent
No one says a word of anything.

A sonorous pendulum swinging
Divides into tiny parts the time
And, her faith in me rocked, my wife
Is nodding off, darning my socks.

Here I lie, my toes to the ceiling,
Feeling in my thoughts the sting.
Oh, dear gods, come to my rescue!
Let me rise quick and sit down to eat.

[*1936?*]

A Pleasant Little Walk

A peasant and his wife playing in the field of life,
and an undressed crowd of people stands on a boat
peering into the deep green water.

The doctor's regaining his strength at the snack bar,
the peasant and his woman splitting under our eyes,
and the doctor rushes back toward the dock.

The steamship stands under the moonlight.
And I am walking by along with Marina,
the weather is so kind to us.

The peasant and his woman are groaning,
under the boat the people moan and drown,
and the doctor is racing back.

[*1935–37*]

* * *

Yes, I'm a poet forsaken by the sky.
Forsaken by the sky from days of old.
But once upon a time Phoebus and I
made a racket joined in a sweet choir.
Yes, there was a time when I and Phoebus
joined in a sweet choir and made a squall.
And there were days when I and Geb were
tight as drops of water in the clouds overhead
and the thunder in its youth rang with laughter.
The thunder rolled flying after Geb and I
pouring from the heavens its golden light.

[*1935–37*]

Once Petrov went for a walk in the forest.
He walked and walked and then he vanished.
Bergson is wondering "Could this be?
Is it for real or is it just me?

Is this a dream or not a dream?"
Looking closer now he sees
Petrov lying in the meadow at ease.
Bergson clambers after him and disappears.

Petrov's head is filled with dread.
"Have I fallen ill or am I mad?
I just saw Bergson melt into thin air.
Am I diseased or just sick in the head?"

[*1936–37*]

* * *

In every church bell there is spite
In every red ribbon there is fire
In every young woman shivering
In every young man his own steed.

[*1936*]

* * *

I love at times to look out of the window
And to observe other people's concerns.
I love at times to look out the window
And through this leave behind my work.
For a long time I stare very intently
Into the face of a young Jewish girl,
Seeking to decipher in her expressions
The regulations of womanly charms.

[*1936–37*]

***

The night sky pales and starts to brighten
Towering above the spire of Peter and Paul,
Through the open window above the leaf piles
The whispering sound of the yardman's broom.
I love to walk homeward dream-enamored,
My sleep-filled body feeling warm the cold,
Rushing through empty streets of the silent,
As though dead, still unpeopled Leningrad.

[*1936*]

* * *

Upon the river floats a boat
That's traveled very very far
And on this boat the sailors four
Are very brave and very broad.

They have two ears upon their skulls
And tails protruding from their bums
And the only thing that scares them
Are little kittens and full-grown cats.

[*1936*]

* * *

The days are fleeing like fleet swifts
And we are flying like little sticks
The clock on the shelf is ticking and
I sit here wearing a wool-knit cap

The days are fleeting like the cups
And we are fleeing like the swifts
The sky is shimmering with lamps
And we are flying like the stars

[*1936*]

* * *

I am incapable of thinking smoothly
My fear gets in the way
It severs my train of thought
As though a ray
Two or even three times each minute
My conscience is contorted by it
I am not capable of action
Only of spiritual angst.

The rain's thunder spoke,
Time has come to a stop.
The clock helplessly tocks.
Grass grow; you have no need of time.
God answer, you have no need of words.

Papyrus flower, how wonderful your calm is.
I also want to be at peace. But all for nothing.

Detskoe Selo, August 12, 1937

* * *

The end is here, my strength expires.
The grave is calling me to my rest.
And suddenly life's trace is lost.

Quieter and quieter beats the heart.
Death races toward me like a cloud
And in the sky the sun's light goes out.

I see death. It's forbidden for me to live.
Good-bye, dear earth! Earth, farewell!

[*1937*]

* * *

We have been killed in the field of life.
Not even a shred of hope remaining.
Our dreams of happiness are over—
The only thing left for us is penury.

[*1937*]

* * *

We—are people
You—are gods
Our villages
Your paths

Detskoe Selo, August 12, 1937

* * *

I was watching a slowly eyelid
that was being lazily lifted
and with its lazy glance
circling the affectionate rivers.

[*after August 13, 1937*]

* * *

You will be murdered by your dreams.
Your interest in this life of struggle will
disperse like the mist. Simultaneously,
the heavenly messenger's wings will miss.
Your wants and desires will wither and wilt
and the inflamed ideas of your youth scatter.
Let them go! Leave them behind, my friend,
your dreams, so your mind is free for the end.

October 4, 1937

Earlier today I will go to bed,
And earlier turn off the lamp,
But I would ask you as well
To wake me earlier tomorrow.

This is simply a delight,
The ease with which I wake!
You just place jam on the table,
I'll awake, in a jiffy, in a blink.
I'll awake, in a jiffy, in a blink,
So as your tea with jam to drink.

November 2, 1937

* * *

This is how hunger begins:
you wake early and full of life
but soon begin to weaken;
the onset of boredom arrives,
the sense of loss impending
of quickening powers of mind,
followed by a peace descending.
And then, the terrifying ending.

[*1937*]

A Very Terrifying Tale

Two brothers walking in the alley
Were finishing up a roll with butter.
Suddenly from around the gutter
A huge dog jumps out barking loudly.

The youngest to the oldest said:
He intends to draw first blood.
So that we don't end up dead
Let's toss him the bread instead.

In the end, all came out smoothly.
The brothers immediately understood
That for every morning stroll
It's best to carry a breakfast roll.

[*1938*]

* * *

A thing of beauty, endearing indeed:
To take away a woman's watch
And give her a memorial bar of soap,
Perfume, a spliff, and a mustache.

March 13, 1938

* * *

Enough of tearing stirrups with my teeth.
The steaming stallion stands under the fir.
Appreciation and rejoicing last a minute
Till again on the balcony the guests stir.

[1938?]

* * *

They shoved me under the table,
But I was very weak and a fool.
The freezing wind blew through
The cracks and landed on my tooth.

It was torturous for me to lie so,
But I was very weak and a fool.
The atmosphere is too cool
For comfort at any time of the year.

I would have lain on the floor in silence,
Flung open my coat of sheepskin wool,
But it became insanely dull to lie so,
For I am very weak and a fool.

April 23, 1938

The Sensual Woodsman

When in the distance flashed saws
And the axes had started ringing,
My girlfriends all became dearer.
I'm in love with them ever since.

Oh, girlfriends, my dear girlfriends,
So pleasant to sense you with my hands!
You're all so smooth! All so solid!
One more wonderful than the next!

It's so pleasant to touch your breasts,
Brush my lips the length of your legs.
Oh, help me people, dear people.
Oh, help me God, my dear God!

August 24, 1938

* * *

I thought of eagles for a long time
and understood such a whole lot:
the eagles soar above the clouds,
they fly and fly and touch no one.
They live on cliffs and on mountains
and are intimate with water sprites.
I thought a long time about eagles
but confused them, I think, with flies.

March 15, 1939

If a state could be likened to the human organism then,
in case of war, I would like to live in its heel.
—Daniil Kharms, 1938